CAPE MAY GHOST STORIES

Book Three

Includes tales of haunted places in

Ocean City   The Wildwoods
...and the South Jersey shore

Charles J. Adams III

EXETER HOUSE BOOKS

CAPE MAY GHOST STORIES
Book Three
by Charles J. Adams III

©2002

Exeter House Books
PO Box 8134
Reading, PA 19603
www.ExeterHouseBooks.com

ISBN 1-880683-16-4

First Edition
June 2002
Printed in the United States of America

All photographs by the author.
All post cards from the collection of the author.

To Lefty, Mabel and Charles Jr.

TABLE OF CONTENTS

FOREWORD

The title of this book says it all: *Cape May Ghost Stories, Book Three*. But notice, please the subtitle: *Includes Tales of Hauntings from Ocean City, The Wildwoods, and the South Jersey shore...*"

For this excursion into the unknown, we have ventured farther north along the eastern barrier islands of Cape May County and into the string of cities and towns that make up what the shoobies' (you know who you are) call "Down the Shore."

Researching a book in midwinter in those places can be difficult. Finding anyone with a story to share is a challenge. In fact, finding anyone at all in January and February along the south Jersey shore can be a daunting task.

If in the bleak midwinter is the worst of times to seek and find ghost stories in summer resort towns, it is also the very best of times.

One is forced to forget the boardwalks and beaches, forego the taffy and tee shirt shops, and forsake all the temptations that these towns offer, even in the coldest, darkest days of the year.

Instead, the researcher finds warmth in the historical societies and libraries, makes connections

1

via email and telephone, and knocks on doors where the "townies"–the real people of these real towns reside.

What follows are stories collected from Cape May Point to the Great Egg Harbor Inlet, with stops in places that could be considered to be far off the beaten tourist trail.

In our continuing quest for ghost stories there were many dead ends (no pun intended), many U-turns, and many drive-through quick stops where stories remained half-told and pitifully incomplete.

Still, it is worth mentioning some of those many stories that tantalize, if only as truncated tales and lingering legends.

There are many such stories that can be grouped in a genre of what we have come to call "They Say" stories. Just who "They" may be is often an elusive proposition. Nevertheless, from place to place, wherever we go to collect our stories, there are plenty of accounts that can only be attributed to a nebulous someone who is as mysterious as the stories they tell.

We endeavor always to secure interviews with those who have had encounters with ghosts, but often cannot either find the right person or secure permission to use the stories.

Such is the case with "Carmen," a ghost that haunts a Cape May County administrative building in Cape May Court House. We were assured that several county employees had brushes with her spirit and at least one other that haunt the basement and mail room areas. *They Say* that on occasion, the faint, plaintive sound of a violin from a fiddling phantom can be heard in those rooms.

Despite several attempts to track down the *they*, they could not be found.

It's much the same story (or non-story) at places such as the old Beasley Estate, near Cape May Court House, where it is said a ghost may have tormented workers on the job refurbishing the place. And, *they say* that a kind, ghostly woman has been seen passing medications inside the county's Crest Haven facility.

Many more stories we have gathered can be attributed to eyewitnesses or credible hearsay, but lack the depth that others may possess.

Included in this genre is the story of the possible haunting of one of the oldest homes in Avalon, the Victorian gem now known as the Sealark Bed & Breakfast.

Described as one of the original great houses on First Avenue in the old Peermont development, the ca. 1891 home is operated by innkeepers Pat Ellis and John Oldham.

The comfortable place has been hosting visitors since the 1940s, when it was first opened as an old-fashioned guesthouse. Ellis and Oldham took possession in 1985 and soon after were advised that something may be awry.

For the first few years of their ownership, the two held down full-time jobs elsewhere and left the weekday management chores to young women.

"All the girls hated to clean this one room, which was the master bedroom on the second floor," Pat Ellis recalled. "They would always say that things would happen, that the door would close and lock behind them, and things like that."

What was odd is that the reports from these college girls came independent of one another. "The girls didn't know each other," Pat continued, "but they all had this sense about that one room, Room 3."

In about 1990, an elderly man stopped by and provided not only much information about the history of the house but a possible baseline and name of whatever spirit may be in Room 3.

The gent told Pat that his great-grandfather had built the house. When he died, his sister, whose name was Rebecca, inherited the house. The man described his great-aunt Rebecca as an elderly spinster who married a Coast Guard captain very late in life.

Then, the story took on a bit of intrigue and mystery.

"The only thing I can tell you," Pat said, "is that Rebecca's body was never found."

Leaving the imagination to fill in the gaps of that story, it is logical to believe that if there is any restless energy in the Sealark, it could be attributed to Rebecca.

"It has become sort of a Sealark joke that whenever anything happens, well, Rebecca is at it again," Pat Ellis said.

4

Regular guests have come to know Rebecca's "antics" well, and Pat just shrugs it all off.

"She's a very nice ghost," she said with a nervous laugh, "she never does anything nasty."

I nside the treasure chest that is the Wildwood Historical Society, we met Bob Bright Sr. and Bob Bright Jr., a father-son team who combed through their collective memories to come up with any and all haunted places of lore in their home town.

The elder Mr. Bright recalled a childhood "haunted house" that was to be avoided at all cost. The abandoned two and one-half story home was in the 300 block of 18th St., between Central and Surf Avenues, he said. Back several decades ago, all but the bravest made a wide berth around the eerie old place that was supposed to be infested with any number of ghouls and goblins.

Bob Bright Jr. spoke of a reputed ghost in the old Wildwood Fire Co. No. 1 on Pine Avenue. That building is long gone and has been replaced by the present firehouse. But, it was in the old structure that a firefighter passed away, and perhaps has never left.

Mr. Bright said that there were often reports of the ghost rambling and rumbling in the third floor lodge room and in the second floor bunkroom in which he died.

A lso in Wildwood, Todd Keininger said that neither he nor wife Natalie have had any untoward experiences as innkeepers of The Sea Gypsy Bed & Breakfast on E. Magnolia Avenue.

5

Nevertheless, Todd did confirm that the place might still harbor a spirit that was reported to them when they bought the building in 1995.

Built around the turn of the 20th century, what is now The Sea Gypsy was an apartment building, and it was in that configuration that a little girl who lived with her family on the first floor claimed she had seen entities in the turret-peaked, verandah-wrapped building.

"She said she had seen a little girl in a Sunday dress," said Keininger. "She had long hair and either ponytails or pigtails."

The great Wildwood Boardwalk yielded a tale told by Anthony Canzano, who had worked briefly at the late, lamented Castle Dracula.

Destroyed by fire the morning of January 16, 2002, the boat ride and walkthrough attraction was a wildly popular fixture of the Boardwalk since 1976, and was among the most famous "dark rides" in the world.

While employed there in the summer of 1998, Canzano heard many stories about the ghost they called "Victoria."

"One night," he told us, "we were playing around with an Ouija board. We got Victoria, who said she had fallen off a steam-powered carousel because a rope came loose. That's all she told us. I think she said it was in the 1920s."

According to Mr. Canzano, "Victoria" would appear to workers only briefly and, in his words, "looked like an old-time movie scene, sort of transparent, if you know what I mean."

He also said workers would spot shadowy forms in certain portions of the castle. These figures that faded in and out of view in places such as the second floor balcony "Red Room" and in the Dungeon were called "shades" by those who witnessed them.

When Marj and John Loeper bought the ca. 1894 Queen Anne house at 401 Wesley Ave. in Ocean City, it was a classic "fixer-upper." Although it was among the first homes to be built up Peck's Beach way, it had fallen on hard times. The Loepers transformed it into the charming Northwood Inn Bed & Breakfast.

John Loeper said that he has no reason to believe the inn is haunted, but there have been others who would disagree.

"We have one room in the house where a couple of our girls are uncomfortable going into after dark or by themselves," he admitted. "More than once, a vacuum cleaner came on all by itself. And, they would often walk out of that room and the light pattern would be different, as if somebody had changed the lights."

Mr. Loeper said he could feel a certain sense of enchantment not only in his B&B, but also in other sections of the historic area of Ocean City in which it is located. It's as if the spirits of the earliest inhabitants of the island are still present.

One particular place is in Memorial Park across the Tabernacle grounds. "There's an aura about that piece

7

of land as you walk across it," he said. "When you walk there, especially at night, there's something about that land that is very special."

In Latin American folklore, a dancing turtle carries the wisdom of the world on its back. At the Dancing Turtle Inn, 424 Wesley Ave. in Ocean City, Arminda and Don Ciancarelli have created their own bit of lore.

Don confided to us right up front that what he was about to tell us was a concoction–a fable fabricated as a tale to tell as a Halloween walking tour coursed past his little inn. Although it is pure fiction, it is so inventive and so delightful that it warrants inclusion here.

The name of the inn piqued our curiosity. How Mr. Ciancarelli explained its origin satisfied that curiosity, sort of:

"At one time," he said with a storyteller's lilt, "when this was barren land and dunes, the turtles would come up to this particular dune, this property, and lay their eggs.

"It became known as 'Turtle Hill.' When they started developing the land and bulldozed the dunes to build houses, this particular house sat right on the old nesting ground.

"It is said that millions of baby turtles were destroyed when they bulldozed here, and when we hear noises in this house, it is the sound of the little ghost turtles."

In truth, Don Ciancarelli and others have heard seemingly unexplainable sounds in the house, but attributes them to the wind, or.....whatever.

Turtles figure, if only abstractly, in another bit of folklore in Cape May County–the day the Revolutionary War came to Two Mile Beach.

At the very southern tip of Wildwood Crest, where the land thins between Sunset Lake and the sea, that land was once split by what was called Turtle Gut Inlet. It was there, in the summer of 1776, that the brig "Nancy" was sailing along the coast loaded with ammunition and supplies for the Continental Army. As she approached Turtle Gut Inlet, a pair of British frigates who were no doubt intent on destroying the ship and its cargo accosted her.

The Nancy attempted to escape through Turtle Gut Inlet, but ran aground. Two nearby American vessels came to her rescue. Sailors from the frigates Wasp and Lexington boarded her and began to offload the cargo while their shipmates manned the guns and returned the British fire.

As the furious action continued, Capt. John Barry of the Lexington came up with a brilliant scheme. He ordered that 50 pounds of gunpowder be packed at the base of the ship's mainsail. As he and his crew abandoned the doomed Nancy, they set fire to the sail.

The British watched as the Americans scurried to shore. They sent a boarding party to the Nancy to douse the flames and claim their prize of war. But, the sail had acted as a fuse and before the British sailors had time to celebrate their "victory" on the deck of the Nancy, the brig–and the Brits–exploded with a blast that was said to be heard as far away as Philadelphia.

John Barry's inventiveness did not go unnoticed, as did not his many other heroics during the war. It was *Captain* Barry who became *Commodore* Barry, who went down in history as the "father of the U.S. Navy" and the namesake of a big bridge over the Delaware River.

The Nancy has been memorialized in the official seal of Wildwood Crest and on the logo of the Wildwood Crest Historical Society.

Do the ghosts of those British sailors haunt the area around Miami and New Jersey avenues, where an historical sign now marks the spot of the bloody conflict? Go there...look...listen...and let us know.

A vintage view of the "Roman Arch" that once welcomed visitors to Wildwood Crest on Pacific Avenue.

10

INTRODUCTION

One more note about the cover of this book. From beach to bay, Cape May County is blessed with boundless beauty. The idea of a cover featuring a montage of "Gingerbread" Victorian inns, quiet beach scenes, or quaint streetscapes crossed our minds.

In the end, we chose a cover illustration that centers on one image: The flame of a candle.

More than any photograph of any familiar place, that picture stands as a symbol.

Since its inception in 1982 and in each of more than two dozen titles, the author and publisher have endeavored to weave threads of history and folklore through the fabrics of each volume that has been published by Exeter House Books.

More than that, in post-publication promotional book signings, lectures, and speeches given by the author, every effort is made to keep alive the ancient art of storytelling.

As is the case in each of its predecessors, this book is not a historical treatise. Nor is this book or any of its Exeter House brethren a work of fiction. No one who contributed a story was compensated, and neither author nor publisher received compensation for those stories.

Similarly, neither author nor publisher has endorsed, lent their names to, or is in any way affiliated with ghost tours or any similar events or attractions.

Those enterprises are doing what Exeter House Books is attempting to do, and it seems to be working.

Just how much a good, old-fashioned ghost story can affect people is illustrated in the thoughts of Cindy Schmucker, innkeeper at the Bedford Inn on Stockton Avenue in Cape May City.

Cindy freely admits she has never had any frightening experiences in her ca. 1881 Victorian Italianate inn.

Crafted from what was built as a double side-by-side home, what was once called The Chelsea became the Bedford when the Bedsworth and Ford families purchased the place in 1966.

The Schmucker family established the Bedford Inn in 1975 after extensive renovations.

"A couple of times I thought there was somebody there when there wasn't," Cindy said, "but I never saw anything."

However, she did confirm that some guests have felt presences and have heard sounds they could not attribute to any natural source.

"I'll tell you what I think happened," Cindy confided. "I think that my guests see the ghost tours pass by. Often, they stop across the street on my block.

"The guests then ask about the tour, or they want to go on it, and then they're more or less susceptible to it.

"But, maybe, who knows? I've definitely had several guests tell me they have heard people walking, or doors closing or opening in the hallways outside their rooms, those kinds of things."

Have those guests been influenced by the ghost tours? Are the bumps they hear in the night products of the power of suggestion?

If so, so be it.

We carefully chose the artwork that graces the cover and back cover of this book.

That solitary flame on the front of this book represents our sincere attempt to keep the fires of folklore and storytelling alive. The photograph of an electrified Cape May streetlight on the back cover is indicative of that city's efforts to bring 19th century charm to the 21st century.

Through these stories within these pages, in tales told in those haunted bed and breakfasts, inns, shop, and private properties; and on those walking tours that course through the "gaslit" streets of Cape May, we encourage generations now and in the future to enjoy these *Ghost Stories of Cape May*.

We have invited you to the campfire, and you have gathered around it. Now, turn the pages and enjoy.

And…sleep tight tonight!

📖

13

GHOSTS FROM BAY TO BEACH

We return once more to the streets of Cape May for a look at what many people will never see–the ghosts that stroll on those streets and in the properties that line them.

In this third volume of ghost stories, we seek and discover tales told by those who *have* seen the spirits and who have agreed to share their experiences with us–and with you.

It is almost amusing that given the number of ghost stories in the incredible assortment of Victorian B&Bs and inns on the tree-shaded and gaslit streets of this magnificent city, there are still those innkeepers who have shied away from allowing their stories of hauntings and the unexplained to be told to the

14

public—even though they will confide, "off the record," that they have had experiences with the unknown in their premises.

This, then, has created an interesting phenomenon.

In the course of researching this, and the first two books of this trilogy, we met about a dozen innkeepers who told us they or their employees or their guests have had brushes with ghosts in their establishments. But, because they thought it would be "bad for business" to have those stories published, they opted to keep the stories to themselves.

What this has created is a sort of "Russian Roulette" for those who come to enjoy the charms of a Cape May B&B.

Is the place haunted? If its story is related in any of these volumes, you know it is. You can read the stories, visit the inns, shops, and restaurants, and perhaps have an encounter of your own.

If it is one of the B&Bs whose owners decided not to allow their stories to be published (but admitted to have had sightings, etc. in their places), you may never know.

However, if all conditions are right, you just might!

You may awaken in the middle of the night to find a glowing form hovering over your bed. You may be shaken from a sound slumber by the sound of a creaking closet door or a shadowy figure darting across your bedchamber.

You may catch the fleeting glimpse of someone—or some*thing*—making its way slowly down a staircase.

Or, you may hear the hollow sound of footsteps just outside your bedroom door.

The next morning, as you gather with the innkeeper for breakfast, you will ask about those visions or those sounds. Then, and only then, they may share their secrets with you.

Secrets? Cape May is bulging with secrets. This series of books has only begun to account for the rich inventory of secrets–of ghost stories–in this fabled city.

To begin this third book, we decided to turn back the pages and revisit some of the haunted places that were mentioned in the first two volumes.

We started just north of the city in the Cape May county seat, Cape May Court House, in which is located the circa-1854 building now known as **The Doctor's Inn**.

The inn's pedigree is described *in Cape May Ghost Stories: Book Two* (pp. 25-29) and our initial findings regarding its hauntings are also detailed in that chapter.

The story is of the ghost of a young girl who romped freely through the inn.

Innkeeper Louis Thompson confirmed for this book that unusual occurrences have continued, and the prospect of the sprightly spirit has drawn interest from serious researchers of the paranormal and curious guests.

"Folks from the South Jersey Ghost Research group have been here twice and investigated," Thompson said, "and they claim that there are actually quite a few ghosts in the house. And, they say that Dr. Wiley's ghost dwells in the basement."

That would be Dr. John Wiley, the namesake of the inn.

Louis Thompson was rather matter-of-fact in his recapitulation of the recurring incidents there.

"I've had a few customers who have had experiences," he confirmed. In one, two people were in room number five and one night the bathroom light kept going on and off.

"I had another guest who was locked out of her bathroom and couldn't get back into it all night."

These incidents, though vexing, are harmless examples of the ghosts' energy entering the electrical system and playing tricks on patrons.

Thompson said many people choose The Doctor's Inn because they have heard of its hauntings. One couple came from as far as Minnesota in hopes of catching a glimpse of, or feeling the presence of, a ghost.

"I, myself, have had one experience," Thompson added. "I left here one evening and left the sliding glass doors out back unlocked. I came back into the house that evening through those doors, bent down, closed the door, locked it, and when I stood up it felt as if I had bumped into someone. But, there was no one there."

As this book was being written, The Doctor's Inn was in the process of expanding a bit by converting Dr. Wiley's office into a guestroom.

One can only imagine, based on the theory that spirit energy is somehow released by alterations to a property, what activity will be released once that conversion is complete.

In *Cape May Ghost Stories: Book One* (pp. 35-40) the shop on the Washington Street Mall was called Keltie's, and it was a bookstore.

That building is now the downtown branch of the Rio Grande landmark Christmas shop, **Winterwood** (which has its own ghost, "Hester"–see *Book One*, pp. 27-29).

Although the name has changed, the haunting hasn't.

Brenda Mathis is manager of the Washington Street Winterwood, and confirmed that just as a pesky spirit wreaked minor havoc in the former bookstore, it does so in the Christmas shop.

"One night we were all at the register and all of a sudden all of the motion detectors started going off," she recalled. That, of course, riled the employees on duty that night. So did the sight of ornaments rising out of boxes and rolling across the floor, and various other unexplainable events that have taken place there.

For the record, they still blame anything untoward that happens in the shop on a ghost they–and the folks in the old bookstore–called "Charlie."

Another spirit we met earlier (*Book Two*, pp. 43-51) maintains a vigil at the **Inn at 22 Jackson**.

She is called "Esmerelda," and even those guests who never read our book have volunteered their stories of strange goings-on in the charming rooms of the B&B.

Innkeeper Barbara Masemore said she has had several reports, and there is a recurring pattern.

"What I'm fascinated by," she remarked, "is that 'Esmerelda' always shows up in the same places and in the same fashion...and I *never* tell the guests about her.

Some may have read the previous accounts and were thus predisposed to a sighting. Many, according to Ms. Masemore, swear they knew nothing of any ghost stories at 22 Jackson until they, themselves, were caught up in them.

The haunted reputation of the inn has not kept people away–hardly. Barbara said she gets several requests for the story and to stay in the room in which most of the activity has taken place.

"We call it the 'Esmerelda Room,'" she said. "But honestly, I never tell the stories because I'm much more interested in hearing what the people will tell *me*."

She is unfazed by the prospect of sharing her home, and her business, with a ghost. "Oh, not at all," she said. "I truly believe there is more than one spirit here. Hey, it's a beautiful place, and in a hundred years, *I'd* come back here!"

On page 11 of *Book One*, the story of the sobbing spirit, the rolling baby carriage, and other phantoms in the **Colvmns by the Sea** (not a typo, they use the Roman "U" in their name) begins.

And, in an interview with employee Bernadette Kaschner, we can confirm that the hauntings have remained strong at the stately seaside inn.

Indeed, if past and present stories are considered, the Colvmns ranks among the most intensely haunted places in Cape May.

Ms. Kaschner is a believer, and for good reason. "I saw a gentleman sitting in the dining room in the summer when it was very hot," she said. "I didn't realize it at first, but he was wearing all this old-fashioned clothing that was so out of place for a day like that."

As that gent seemed to come out of nowhere and disappear back into it, another apparition crossed paths with Bernadette not much later.

"I also saw a lady walking in my kitchen. She was wearing a long gray skirt with a gray jacket and I think she may have been one of the maids who used to work here," she ventured.

"That day, when I saw her, I actually ran after her because I couldn't imagine who she was or why she was there," she continued.

But, her brief chase was to no avail, as the mysterious visitor vanished right before her eyes.

A while later, Bernadette happened upon an elderly relative of a former owner of the old mansion. "I asked him what the maids back in the old days used to wear," she said. "I never told him exactly why I wanted to know," she added. But, her suspicions were confirmed when he described to a "T" what she had seen in phantom form crossing through her kitchen that day.

"People see things here all the time," she said.

The ghostly ledger is long at the Colvmns.

In Room 8, one may discover the giggling spirit of a young girl who has been heard by several guests.

Room 10 seems to be occupied by an elderly man whose restless spirit strolls in and out of the room on no particular timetable. This rambunctious wraith has also been spotted in a third floor parlor. One time, a guest who also happened to be an artist saw the ghost. "He drew a picture of the old man," Bernadette said, "and he showed it to my daughter. Later, my daughter found an old picture of a former owner of the place, and it looked just like him."

That artist/guest could never have seen that photograph, as it was secreted deep within the confines of a private office.

Guests and employees have often caught the pungent aroma of a puff of cigar smoke that comes out of nowhere. Bernadette constantly hears footsteps from unseen feet, and several guests claim they have smelled the sweet scent of fresh roses in a second floor parlor–when there were no roses in that second floor parlor.

There is the occasional downside to all of this, admitted Ms. Kaschner. "We've had guests check out early because they have spotted a spirit," she said.

But generally, those who have an unexpected encounter take it with grace and a sense of adventure.

Bernadette tried to explain the recurring phenomena of the ghosts at the Colvmns by the Sea, but she is at wit's end to do so.

"People ask me if what we see are 'ghostly-looking,' if you know what I mean. They're always amazed when I tell them that what I've seen are solid people, so to speak, just like us."

So to speak.

The grand Washington Street estate known now as **The Southern Mansion** was the subject of a peculiar ghost story in *Book Two*, pages 21-23.

And, according to front desk clerk and tour manager Jean Smith, the spirit they call "Esther" continues to make her presence known there.

Esther was the lady of the house, they say, from the 1880s through the 1940s, and many tales are told about her afterlife antics.

Smith has another story...that came from what could be considered an unlikely source.

"I came on duty one morning about eight o'clock," he said. "A woman who had been a nun for about 27 years had been on duty overnight, and when I got in I asked her how everything went."

With that question, that former nun was anything but, uh, nun-ly as she greeted Smith with a steel stare and stern instructions.

"Look at the log book," she uttered.

A confused Jean Smith responded. "I asked her what she meant and she repeated, 'LOOK AT THE LOG BOOK!'

"I opened the log book and, it just said 'Esther,' and the date.

"I asked her what happened. She said she had been asleep on a cot next to the front desk. There had been a wedding there the previous day and the bride came to her, feeling ill."

The former nun administered care to the bride, and returned to her nocturnal duty.

"In the middle of the night," Smith continued, "she said there was a very gentle rapping on the door. She awoke and could see it was dark in the front desk area but there was light coming in from the corridor.

"She could see two little feet. There was somebody standing outside the door. So, she got up, put a robe on, went to the door, opened it, and...there was no one there!"

The overnight clerk thought it might have been someone from an adjacent room or someone in the front sitting room. But, a check revealed that there was nobody nearby at all.

"On a hunch," Smith said, "she opened the front door and looked out on the porch. Again, nobody. The whole first floor was deserted.

"Then, she looked at her watch and it was just a few minutes after three o'clock. She said, 'Oh, my God' when it dawned on her that when that rap had come on the door it was exactly 3:05 a.m., and that was the time of day she was born and it was thus her birthday.

23

"She felt that Esther had come to wish her a happy birthday."

If that all seems to be a bit of a stretch, re-read the original account of "party girl" Esther's perambulations in the Southern Mansion.

Jean Smith was more amused than anything by his colleague's story, until he went into the kitchen that day for a cup of coffee. There, he met some staff members who told him that there was evidence that Esther had been in the kitchen area the previous night. They told him glasses had been broken and other signs were left that her playful ghost had come to call.

What's more, and it was news to Mr. Smith, they said Esther's ghost always seems to appear following a wedding or party in the elegant mansion.

There may be another reason Esther wanders eternally through The Southern Mansion.

"I have heard that she appears frequently in the basement of our new wing, which was constructed in 1996-97," he said.

Never to take these reports at face value, Smith questioned why her ghost might ramble in that new wing.

That question may have been answered when an old-timer at the mansion told him the wing was built on the site of Esther's beloved rose garden.

"Certainly," Smith concluded, "Esther is still with us. She's very much a part of the personality of the house, and we're glad to have her."

Our updates of stories in the two previous ghost books took an unusual turn in a letter received from an individual who claimed to have had a most incredible meeting with a most unexplainable entity near the very tip of Cape May.

It relates to the story of "Puss" Williams' experience with a mysterious being in the countryside of Cape May County (*Book One*, pp. ix-x).

The letter writer, who asked that his name not be used because of the sensitive nature of his profession, said he was raised on the west side of the Wharton tract. "Day and night I had wandered, camped, cycled, and canoed through the woods of South Jersey since I was a small boy," he added. "There was nothing about or in those woods which I feared."

He had doubtlessly heard the legends of the Jersey Devil and other mythical or mystical creatures said to inhabit the Pine Barrens and other forests of South Jersey, but he pooh-poohed them as he became one with nature.

All that changed a bit in late spring, 1981, when he and a friend had a compelling and confusing experience in the bird refuge at **Cape May Point**.

It was the "Puss" Williams story in *Book One* that sparked his memory and spurred him to write.

"At the time," he said, "I was nearly forty. Both my friend and I were veterans of a profession where we might meet and need to swiftly counter dangerous situations on a daily basis, without panic or over-reaction."

Even with that training and inner strength, what happened that day near sunset on a pathway at Cape May Point remains etched indelibly in both of their memories.

"The path is a labyrinthine boardwalk winding to a large pond at the center. The path leads to a wooden deck at one edge of that pond. The hike in takes about twenty minutes. My friend and I walked to this deck and stopped to talk for a while. What happened next still gives me a chill to remember it.

"As we talked, paying more attention to each other than the surroundings, both she and I became aware of *something* on the far side of the pond.

"It was big...possibly seven or eight feet tall. It was in a place that should have been drenched with the slanting light of the nearly setting sun, but it was...*dark*...like the total absence of light.

"I felt a malicious intelligence focused on us from that...that *thing*. It was shapeless, but it was *there!*"

Both the correspondent and his friend were stopped dead in their tracks.

"In a very quiet voice," he continued, "my friend said, 'Do you see that?'

"'Yes', I said.

"Realizing that all the birds had grown silent and that the sun would soon set, I said, 'I think it's time to go.'

"Without further discussion, I led off, prepared to defend against...*what?* She followed, covering our rear.

"The walk out was tense. My every sense was alive. I heard no animals. We were not even molested by mosquitoes. Twenty minutes later, as the setting sun touched the horizon, we broke into the clear. Outside the bird sanctuary, the song of evening wildlife could again be heard.

"We looked at each other and walked side by side to the car."

And, the adventure was over. But, it lives on in his and her minds.

"My friend and I see each other from time to time," he added. "Every once in a while, in a different voice, one of us starts to say, 'Do you remember...?'

"'Yes, I do,' the other will quickly respond."

And forever, they shall.

The **Sea Holly Inn** has gone through a change of ownership since our last book, but one thing remains constant at the Stockton Avenue B&B–its hauntings.

That's hauntings, as in plural, because two primary entities and quite possibly one or two more have been detected at the Gothic style inn where the likes of Marlene Dietrich and other stars of the past once stayed.

In *Book Two* (pp 55-59), we wrote about then-innkeeper Christie Igoe's experiences, as well as the findings of sensitives who called at the Sea Holly to see what *they* could see.

We update the story with more recent investigations that have more than substantiated Christie Igoe's earlier experiences.

The innkeepers are now Walt and Patti Melnick, and when they purchased the property, its resident ghosts came along in the deal.

Although the affable Mr. Melnick professes to not believe in ghosts, he is at a loss trying to explain some of the odd occurrences some guests, all psychic investigators—and even he has reported.

One case in particular centered on a baby monitor they placed at the front entrance. It was there to pick up sounds such as the door opening and guests entering.

Those natural sounds aside, the monitor would occasionally rustle with the barely distinct sounds of muffled voices. They spoke sentences, engaged in conversation. Never, though, could the exact nature of the conversations be understood. And, when anyone would venture forth to the front door immediately upon hearing the voices, they would find no source whatsoever of the conversations.

Walt also told a researcher that he was very uncomfortable going on the third floor of the inn after nine o'clock at night—even if he was a non-believer in all that supernatural silliness.

So, what rooms and where in the Sea Holly Inn harbor spirit activity? Pick and choose!

In the process of probing the activity at the inn, investigators concluded that the hauntings occur in the main room, the hallway to the kitchen, Room 4, Room 7, Room 8, and, oh yes, Room 9.

That's in addition to the entryway, a back staircase, and...the third floor, Mr. Melnick.

Just who are those investigators who determined that the Sea Holly is indeed haunted?

Among them was Jane Doherty, a one-time high school English teacher who is now listed as a "psychic, ghostbuster, lecturer, and hypnotist."

The South Plainfield, New Jersey-based woman has been interviewed on major television networks, and has been featured in national magazines and newspapers.

It was at former innkeeper Christie Igoe's behest that Ms. Doherty visited the Sea Holly to sort out psychic fact from fancy.

Armed with previous accounts of strange sightings and voices that came out of nowhere, she first gathered all available information that may help to identify or quantify the mysteries of the inn.

One very curious manifestation was that of the faint but discernible image of a woman who was seen standing between a bride and groom who were married at the Sea Holly. In one particular wedding picture, this strange form was clearly seen, although all that were present at the ceremony agreed there was no such woman standing there at the time.

According a report on Jane Doherty's web site, that invisible interloper who manifested herself only on the photograph may have been identified through a harrowing encounter Jane had when she stayed overnight in a room on the second floor of the B&B.

It was about four in the morning when Jane was awaked to the eerie sound of a squeaking bed frame. As she cleared her thoughts, she then felt the distinct sensation that someone had sauntered up to the bed and lay next to her. Her first reaction was to verbally instruct the ethereal intruder to go away.

And, go away it did, until around dawn when another sound and a strange shaking motion rustled her awake once more.

"Again she felt someone lay next to her," a report on the matter declared. "Only this time, she knew it was a male spirit. He kept calling a woman's name. Paralyzed by fear, Jane hoped he did not think she was his wife."

The drama played out through the early morning hours. Jane started hearing the voice of a man, and then a woman. Their conversation from the "other side" grew more intense and argumentative.

Through it all, Jane reasoned that the female voice was that of a young servant who resided in the house and was to marry a wealthy relative of a former owner of the house.

Tragically, the woman died just before her wedding day.

It is her ghost, Jane concluded, that haunts that section of the building, and it was her image that was captured in the wedding pictures–an image triggered by the joyous event that took place at the Sea Holly and a joyous event the deceased young woman was never to experience.

In other readings of the house by other psychics, the spirits of a young girl, at least one other young woman, and an enigmatic chap they've come to call the "Sea Captain" have been identified.

One researcher who employs more technical than psychical methods in his investigations picked up what are called "electronic voice phenomena" (EVPs) in the inn.

Sure enough, these snippets of sound that were deposited on tapes from equipment that was left on the "record" mode during the silent nights at the inn purportedly included the quick but identifiable voice of a young girl and an older man.

Kenny Biddle, the electronic investigator, said the voices were the clearest and most conclusive EVPs he had ever retrieved.

On the tape could be heard, especially when isolated and slowed down, the sound of a little girl saying "I wanna go out and play." Ever so briefly, the sad appeal came and went sometime during the night.

And later on the tape, another voice–a voice tinted by the brogue of what could well be considered a grizzled man of the sea–was heard.

Although what the man uttered was not nearly as crisp as the little girl's plea, it seemed as if he blurted out, for whatever reason, "He rowed back!."

Could the younger ghostly voice be that of a little girl who died too young and calls out to anyone who may hear? Could her forlorn spirit be seeking, always in vain, a playmate who will release her from her eternal shackles? Could she really have been an Irish immigrant lass named "Kathleen," as they have come to call her?

Could the old man be forever lamenting a tragedy at sea? Could he really have been named Captain Rodgers, as they have come to call him?

These are among the many unanswered and intriguing mysteries at the Sea Holly Inn.

This is not to say that folks haven't tried to solve those mysteries over the last few years.

Among the eminent psychics who have found the Sea Holly to be fascinating fodder for their pursuits is Craig McManus, from Ho-Ho-Kus, New Jersey.

In fact, Walt Melnick credits McManus with cracking one particular mystery in his lovely inn.

"It all started in February, 2001," Walt remembered. "Craig was sitting in the parlor and he told me we had a little Irish girl named Kathleen on the third floor."

The revelation emerged from a séance held at the Sea Holly and led by McManus. In that session, he said he could hear the giggly voice of a little girl calling "Mama…mama!"

A few months after that psychic declaration, Kenny Biddle joined the search and his EVPs seemed to support the location and nature of the haunting.

"I got the sense it was a young child," Craig McManus concluded. "She was the daughter of a servant. That's where the activity is coming from–not from the mother, but from her child.

"I was thinking perhaps the child died and eventually the mother died. I think it is the spirit of the child who shakes the bed, calling for her mother."

McManus believes the eternal bedside beckoning may be the girl's attempts to awaken her mother either from a deep sleep...or death.

The Melnicks' tenure as innkeepers has been quite remarkable from a supernatural point of view.

In an 18-month period following their purchase of the place, 20 guests–all women–have reported the shaking bed phenomenon.

"The first three times it happened," Walt Melnick said, "I had no inkling of what was going on. Three different women came to me in the morning and told me that they had been awakened in the middle of the night by the bed noticeably shaking."

Walt pooh-poohed it at first, but then saw certain patterns emerge–only certain rooms and only women were affected. One quizzical guest, the husband of one of the women who reported the shaking of the bed, went as far as taking the bed apart in a (vain) attempt to find the mechanism that someone, he thought, must have installed to create the shaking effect!

Those points, coupled with Craig McManus' findings, began to create a clearer focus for whatever was happening in the Sea Holly.

Then, a series of events of almost blockbuster proportions added more and more validity to the mental and mechanical discoveries.

In a dark recess of one of the rooms, a hand-colored, Victorian-era photograph was found. While it had to have been in the house when the Melnicks moved in, Walt swore he had never seen it before in his life. Still, it emerged as if by fate.

It was a picture of a lovely woman and her sweet, little daughter. Scrawled in pencil on the back of the framed picture were the words *Mom and Katie, Cape May, 1891.*

Katie? Kathleen? The possibilities are tantalizing.

Tantalizing, too, is an episode Walt remembers when a woman and her elderly mother came down in the morning after spending a night in the Sea Holly.

"They came down for breakfast and asked me to tell them any stories about ghosts in the house. I told the woman the stories, but her mother spoke only Italian, so she didn't understand. The younger woman was translating for her mother.

"The following week, the woman called me. She felt that she had to tell me something. She told me that when she was translating the stories for her mother, she hadn't said anything at the time.

"But later, she said, her mother told her that when they were in their room, she had seen the figure of a little girl, dressed in white, with wings."

Again, Walt was staggered by the call. He reasoned that if the woman cared enough to call him so long after their stay, the experience must have been profound enough to have made a lasting impression.

Although Craig McManus employs his mind in his quest for information, he will occasionally dabble in the electronic side of "ghost hunting."

One time at the Sea Holly, he had placed tape recorders in one particular area in an effort to secure an EVP. What followed could well have been an example of how the two very diverse investigative approaches may have merged.

"We started to smell a really strong scent," McManus remembered. "I wondered if there were flowers around *(there were not)* or a bathroom freshener *(no)*.

"We opened the door to go into the hallway and it was even stronger. And, as we moved around to the front of the house it got very strong and we opened the door to where the tape recorder was and it was as if somebody had smashed a perfume bottle *(they had not)*.

"It was sickeningly strong. In all the years I've done psychic readings, I've gotten some fragrances, but never like this. This was textbook stuff!"

He went back to the room to retrieve the tape recorder, and as he began to rewind the tape, the aroma suddenly dissipated. It simply stopped.

Then, as he played back the tape, the somewhat distorted, creepy, high-pitched voice of a young girl could be heard saying what sounded very much like *"I want to go out and play!"*

Katie? Kathleen?

Could this long-lost photograph depict the ghostly presences at the Sea Holly Inn? On the back of the picture are the words "Mom and Katie, Cape May, 1891"

Something should be made abundantly clear. The Sea Holly Inn is a warm, wonderful inn in the highest Cape May tradition. Every room is lovely, and the Melnicks are more friends than innkeepers to all who choose to stay there.

Thanks to a quirky gap in beachfront development, there is an ocean view from the front rooms, and the location is a short walk from the beach and a comfortable distance from the seasonal congestion and noise of downtown Cape May.

Maybe that ocean view keeps the ghost of the old sea captain content. Maybe the love the Melnicks and their predecessors poured into the old house keeps mom and Katie content.

The ghosts there are gentle–quite probably those of a mother and her child.

Which reminds me–the first weekend in 1999 the Melnick's opened their pride and joy inn for guests?

Mother's Day weekend, of course.

TIME FLIES AT TRADEWINDS

These days, it's a funky shop that overlooks the gazebo in the park along Lafayette Street near Jackson.

Long ago, however, the building that houses a shop called Tradewinds was a changing house on the beach. Nobody's exactly sure when it was moved to its present location, but most who work at the cozy store are certain they share the place with an invisible but possibly irascible energy force.

Rachel Fisher had been employed there only a few months before she was introduced to the entity. She had been a friend and steady customer of the owner of Tradewinds long before she started working there on evening and morning shifts in the summer of 2001.

"The first thing I experienced," she said, "is when I was cleaning off the shelves and I was moving things around. I got the distinct feeling that somebody was standing behind me.

"When I turned around, I saw something in the corner of my eye. I saw it. It was a figure. It was rather dark when I saw it, but I knew it was there."

Rachel looked a bit closer, trying to focus on the shadowy form, and it vanished. But then, she began to sense a certain coldness, a certain uneasiness.

"It was strange," she continued. "I thought, OK, maybe because I was by myself, I was just a little scared."

That fear heightened when a bell behind her began to ring. She was startled, but maybe a bit relieved. The bell signaled someone entering the room from an upstairs office area.

"Then," Rachel remembered, "I heard somebody coming down the stairs. I thought maybe it was Lissy (the shop owner) coming back.

"I looked all around back there, though, and there was no one there."

39

Thus ended Rachel's first experience with the unseen intruder at the Tradewinds. But, there is more–much more.

"A couple of weekends later," she added, "I was standing at the cash register. I was checking a customer out. There was a little wind-up alarm clock on a shelf against the wall."

That, of course, was unremarkable. But what became quite remarkable is that Rachel was suddenly distracted by the unlikely and unsettling sight of the clock leaping from the shelf and two or three feet into the store!

"I looked up, and that little clock just jumped up and went into a bowl," she said.

"The customer looked at me, and I at her, and we stood amazed."

Rachel had, early on, become resigned to the possibility that the little shop was haunted.

After the "leaping clock" episode, Rachel mentioned her encounters to the boss–cautiously.

"I asked her if she had any experiences in the store," Rachel said.

Sure enough, the owner, Lissy Fritz, confirmed that similar incidents had played out there, and that particular alarm clock had been the focal point of several of them.

Rachel soon shared her stories with other employees there, and nearly all of them–cautiously–had their own tales to tell.

The former bathhouse has been the subject of several "readings" by sensitives who have confirmed what they can best describe as an "uneasy" spirit there.

Despite that, and despite the shadowy figure and the flying clock Rachel Fisher encountered, she continued to divide her time between there and her teaching job upstate.

As for the possibility–nay, probability–that at the Tradewinds shop she works amidst ghosts, Rachel is nonchalant.

"I grew up in a haunted house," she noted. "I have no problem."

A full moon is suspended in the night sky over the Ocean City Music Pavilion in this early 20th century view.

"HELLO, GRANNY!"

L issy Fritz, whom we met in the last story as the proprietor of the Tradewinds store on Lafayette Street, is cognizant of and comfortable with the spirits that have manifested themselves in her businessplace.

That could well be because she has had another ghostly encounter at another location–her own home.

And, although it was far removed from the "flying clock" in her store, that encounter did involve a timepiece.

It was in January, 1985, about four in the morning. It was in a circa 1920 home on Pearl Avenue in West Cape May.

"I was asleep," Lissy remembered, "but all at once I sat up in bed. I know exactly what time it was because I looked, and the clock read four o'clock."

The glow from the alarm clock wasn't the only thing Lissy saw in the middle of that fateful night.

"I saw my grandmother standing at the foot of my bed," she said. "She didn't say anything. She simply placed her right hand on the bedpost...and was gone!"

In the instant that the vision appeared, and just as it vanished, Lissy managed to fully recognize her grandmother and utter, ever so innocently, "Hello, Granny!"

She is, to this day, ill equipped to explain or understand the ever-so-brief visitation by her "granny's" apparition.

"It was very brief," she lamented, "but very, very clear."

Lissy managed to go back to sleep, but shortly after she awakened the next morning, she would receive a telephone call that would rattle her to her very being.

The call came from her sister, and it was not good news.

Lissy's sister relayed the tragic information that a close relative had passed away in her home in Pennsylvania.

That relative was Lissy's grandmother.

What could have drawn Lissy Fritz' grandmother's spirit to her bedside that night? Was it a sign? A final farewell?

She had never, while alive, been to that West Cape May house. But, the bed in which Lissy slept–the bed to which her "granny" made that eerie visit–once belonged to and was given to Lissy by...her grandmother.

"I still miss her, every day," she confided. "I'd love to see her once more."

43

ART IMITATES THE AFTERLIFE AT THE "HAUNTED" MANSION

Many years ago, Shirley Long was quite content operating a bridal and gift shop on the Washington Street Mall in central Cape May.

Business boomed. Shirley was able to handle virtually every one of a bride's needs for an elegant wedding.

Shirley could do nothing more, however, than suggest a place for the reception following the ceremony.

In the late 1980s, she and husband Ron Long purchased a dilapidated old building at 513 Lafayette Street with the intent of renovating it into a luxurious facility for wedding receptions and social functions.

The building had seen its better day, most folks thought. But, the Longs saw potential there, and worked hard to stabilize and restore it.

After they opened their new venture and sought direction, they allowed a friend to create a dinner-theater operation inside.

The concept caught on quickly, and Elaine's Haunted Mansion Restaurant was born.

44

The showplace has become one of Cape May's biggest attractions, and has been featured in television shows, newspaper and magazine articles, and travel guides.

It is, ostensibly, a smoke-and-mirrors "haunted" attraction where actors and actresses play the ghosts and special effects play with guests' minds.

But, unbeknownst to Ron and Shirley Long when they established their "haunted" attraction, there was much more going on far behind the contrived sets and scenarios. Little did they know that their "haunted" restaurant was, well, *haunted*.

The first sightings or sensings of spirit energy inside Elaine's Haunted Mansion Restaurant could hardly be taken seriously.

After all, the production companies had worked very hard to create an unearthly, eerie environment that would scare the bejeebers out of any and all who attended the dinner shows. Likewise, the cast members were well schooled on how to raise the hackles on the back of the guests' necks.

So, when the occasional patron or employee claimed they had seen or heard something out of the ordinary, it was often dismissed as the work of an overactive imagination teased by the props and plots.

The growing number of reports of ghostly activity—as well as their genuine love for the property—prompted the Longs to dig a bit deeper into the history of the building.

They found that it was built during the Civil War as the resort home of a Philadelphia doctor. They found that, at least in historical hearsay, that doctor had a daughter who was an invalid, and to accommodate that young girl, an elevator had been installed in the home.

That elevator, or what remains of it, will play a major role in the stories that have spun from the real haunting of the "haunted" restaurant.

"I've read all the books about ghosts, I've seen all the programs," Ron Long said. "But what's interesting about the ghost in our building is that it is an entity that seems to talk to people and relate to people.

"Usually, ghostly activity seems to be out there in the ether," he continued. "Our ghost is not like that."

It may seem that Mr. Long is talking about the contrived ghosts created by the production companies at Elaine's.

He is not. He is talking about the *real* ghost there.

"The first time I saw the ghost was in the middle of winter on the second floor," he recalled.

At that time, that area of the building was being used as a storage area.

"I was walking up the steps at about eleven o'clock at night to get something up there. As soon as I got to the top of the steps, I felt as if I was interrupting someone, as if I had walked into somebody.

"I looked up, and all the way down the hall I saw a pattern of lights, just like something out of a ghost movie. It came out of the wall, a long, vertical stream of colored lights. It moved across the room and stopped. Then, it went through the wall and into another room."

Stunned and confused, Ron stood amazed at what he had witnessed.

The encounter drove him to more closely examine the area from which those unearthly lights had emanated.

That area was a void in the building—the empty shaft that once held the long-removed elevator.

It is from or near that cavity that nearly all of the ghostly sightings have originated.

Ron Long is quick to explain that it hasn't been only he, production members, customers, and employees who have witnessed the phenomena.

"One of my favorite stories is from the time the restaurant manager, the chef, and I were up in the front room we call the 'haunted mansion.' It was the middle of the day, and a guy walked in through the kitchen. He was mumbling something and appeared quite jittery. I figured he was some salesman, so I asked if I could help him."

With that, Ron remembered, the man's mumbling became cohesive words. He said, in simplest terms, that he had seen a ghost.

With full knowledge that this visitor could not have been predisposed to expect to see a phantom there, Ron quizzed him.

The man—actually a meat deliveryman—nervously told Ron that a woman—"a woman in an old-fashioned dress," as he described her—had brushed past him, seeming to glide, not walk. He said the woman turned her face toward him, affixed a short stare, and vanished.

"It scared the hell out of the guy," Ron chuckled.

There are those at Elaine's who *are* predisposed to the unexpected there. After all, they work very hard and are quite successful at creating bizarre special effects, psychological thrills and chills, and a real sense that the "Haunted Mansion" is haunted.

But, these members of the show's cast and crew know perhaps more than anyone the line between reality and fantasy.

"I've seen the ghost countless times," said Ron Long. "We've had delivery people, customers, production crew members, you name 'em...see the ghost.

"One of the things that happens a lot is that there are certain seats from which people will come and tell the bartender they'd seen the ghost.

"They all see the same thing, and what they see says the same thing, or same kinds of things, to people."

And, the spirit is most likely to be seen at, near, or coming to or from the old elevator shaft.

That having been established, the folks at Elaine's have, as residents or workers at haunted sites are wont to do, given the ghost a name.

For no historical or factual reason, they call their ghostly girl "Emily."

"She seems a bit melancholy," Ron noted. "She never bothers anybody, never really scares anybody, but everyone who has seen a ghost here describes it the same way."

Furthermore, although there is no real basis to do so, Ron believes the ghost is that of the doctor's invalid daughter. Although her illness or handicap restricted her travels in life, she wanders freely and effortlessly through her old home in the afterlife.

As word of the stories of the ghost at Elaine's spread through the paranormal probing and psychic community, both those who work with their minds and those who work with technological gadgets have descended upon the restaurant to "read" its energies. Both kinds of investigators have discovered enough evidence to confirm that the place is truly inhabited by much more than a contrived spirit or two.

Throughout the "Haunted Mansion" season, throngs descend upon Elaine's to be titillated and tempted by the fabrication of phantoms.

Little do some of them know that lurking just over their shoulders, just out of their peripheral vision, somewhere near certain seats of the room, is the real deal–Emily.

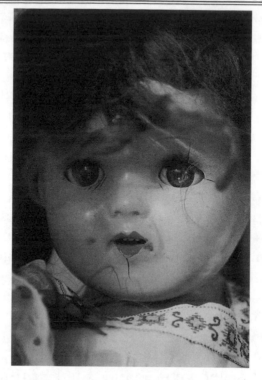

OH, YOU *BOO*-TIFUL DOLL!

L aurie Crookston Johnson's wonderful little doll shop in the Washington Commons Mall is not the kind of place you'd expect to find much ghost activity. The building is relatively new and the business is brisk enough to keep even the most adventurous spirit at bay.

So, there's not much to report at Laurie's "Oma's Doll Shop."

But, the lifelong resident of Cape May has tales to tell about the previous location of the shop, a building on Jackson Street.

Laurie opened her shop in the old place and noticed that the curtains in the front windows of the third floor of the building were tattered, drooping, and disheveled. Not a nice image for the upscale doll shop she had opened on the ground floor, she thought.

For whatever reason, she was told, that third floor was totally inaccessible except for an elaborate placement of ladders and a lot of crawling and climbing. She would tackle the job later.

Oddly enough, the very next day as she looked up to those third floor windows, the curtains were neat and tidy. It was as if someone had somehow gone up to the third floor and straightened things out.

Certain that the owner of the building had done the job, she thanked him. But, he was puzzled. He assured her in no uncertain terms that he, nor anyone he knew of, had not–and could not have–performed that task.

That bizarre incident was followed in short order by another more personal incident in her shop.

It was a pleasant autumn day in Cape May, moderate to near warm temperatures. It was shirtsleeve weather.

"A woman came into the store," Laurie remembered, "she was looking at paper dolls. I remember vividly that she had a long coat on, with a hood. I thought that was odd, because it wasn't cold outside."

The woman was in the middle of the store when Laurie turned her attention away from her for a second or two. When she looked back to ask the oddly clad customer if she could be of assistance, the hooded woman was gone–vanished.

Several people witnessed several strange events in the old Jackson Street store.

On one occasion, a woman came in to pick up a doll she had purchased earlier in the day. But, to Laurie and the customer's chagrin, that doll was nowhere to be found.

Laurie searched everywhere for the missing doll, but to no avail.

But then, she received some unexpected help from her mother, a firm believer in ghosts and that the Jackson Street building was haunted. She claimed to have communicated with the spirit, and even gave it a name–Lucille.

"My mom just blurted out, 'OK, Lucille, where's the doll?'

"Well, with that," Laurie continued, "the doll just slid out from underneath the table, right in the middle of all of us!"

Laurie said she had previously looked under that same table, and saw nothing. But, several people bore witness to the strange happening.

Research has revealed that at one time the doll shop on Jackson Street may have been home to "dolls" of another sort. Local lore has it that the building was once, in Laurie's words, "a house of ill repute."

They say that one of the ladies of the night lived on the third floor and, stung by one of the pitfalls of her profession, gave birth in her upstairs room.

Attempting to keep the birth secret, she was unattended by medical help and the baby died shortly after drawing its first breath.

It wasn't much of a leap for Laurie to reason that maybe, just maybe, the ghosts that inhabit the old building may be that of the young woman and the dead baby, and that both had a certain affinity for dolls.

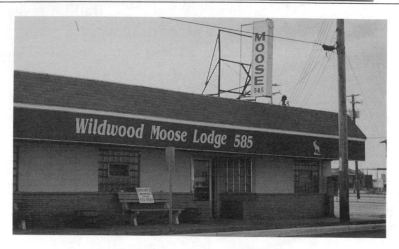

ONCE A MOOSE,
ALWAYS A MOOSE

What, you say? An unusual title for a chapter in a book of ghost stories?

Allow me to explain.

As in any resort town in South Jersey, there are the boardwalks and beaches, hotels and honky-tonks, and the spots where the men, women, girls, and boys of summer spend their time and money.

But, there also those parts of town, those places in those towns, where the tourists rarely tread.

Those places are the backbones of those towns–the places that make Ocean City, the Wildwoods, and Cape May more than just summer resorts.

Such a place in North Wildwood is the Moose Lodge #585.

54

Built in 1949 at 314 Spruce Ave., the one-level social hall is adjacent to a vacant lot that was once packed with vacationers when Ed Zaberer's "World Famous Restaurant" stood there.

Since that attraction burned to the ground in the early 1990s, things are relatively quiet up around the Moose lodge.

Except, that is, for the occasional cavorting of the lodge's resident ghost, Charlie.

There seems to be a plethora of ghost stories that center on a spook by the name of Charlie. As are "Lizzie," "Emily," and "Mary" on the distaff side, "Charlie" is one of the default names given to otherwise unidentified spirits.

At the North Wildwood Moose lodge, however, "Charlie" is very easily identified.

He is identified in yellowing, fragile newspaper clippings in the lodge scrapbook. He can be seen in a framed photograph on a wall.

And, he makes his presence known often, and to many, in the big hall where the locals gather.

At least that's the general consensus among the many Moose members who knew Charlie in life–and those who know him only in his present manifestation.

He is–notice the present tense there–Charlie Kiesel, and there's hardly a soul in the lodge who won't admit that the kindly chap is still hanging around the place that was so much a part of his life.

Charlie's daughter, Barbara Molnar, doesn't discount for a moment the probability that her father's spirit is still present there.

"It tickles me, more or less," she said. "I think, well, yes, he probably is there because it was his place. He just lived to go to the Moose and enjoy himself there. He was quite a fellow."

The Rio Grande woman added that in addition to the socialization the lodge hall provided her father, he would always be tinkering there, involving himself in one project after another.

And, by all accounts at the lodge today, he probably still is.

Letty Fitzpatrick, who transplanted to North Wildwood from North Jersey in the 1970s, is a true believer that Charlie's pesky presence remains strong at Lodge #585.

"He was one of the highest orders of the Moose, and we all believe he's still here," she said.

"People have heard footsteps, sometimes going out the front door, sometimes going out the back. We've looked everywhere and there was nobody there."

Most of the ethereal offerings at the lodge are of, shall I say, the "garden variety" of ghostly goings-on–standard stuff like lights or electrical gadgets going on and off.

But, there are other occurrences that are more singular to the lodge and to Charlie Kiesel himself.

Letty pointed to decorations and beer promotional signs that hang from the ceiling. "They'll spin," she said. "Not all at one time, and not all of them. Maybe it'll be just one of them, spinning around for no reason."

There are no vents, no breezes, no simple explanations for how or why the signs will spin. Often, the spinning has been witnessed by one person who was alone in the room, making it difficult for them to explain to others. But, enough "others" have had it happen to them that virtually everyone who spends any time in the lodge will corroborate the tales of their colleagues.

Quite possibly, the most telling of all incidents there is the unexplained opening and closing of one particular door.

"I have been here with two others at the bar," Letty said, "when *that* door has opened and slammed." She motioned to one particular door that shares a wall with a TV, a dartboard, a massive moose head, and the pictures of three lodge "Pilgrims," the "founding fathers" of the family fraternity.

One of those Pilgrims is Charlie Kiesel. And, the door that has so often opened and closed on its own is the door to "Pilgrim Hall," in which Charlie would have spent much time. "*Much* time," Letty quipped.

"The door didn't just open and blow closed," she pointed out. "The handle turned, the door opened, and then it slammed shut quickly. There was nobody around, and it could not have opened on its own, no way."

Just about anyone around the sweeping bar of the lodge will attest to Letty's stories, but one gent in particular refuses to discuss the matter at all.

What's more, he refuses to stay at the lodge alone. And he, ironically enough, is the administrator.

So, while that individual was mute on the subject (although later overheard talking about his own experiences with Charlie), others were quite vocal.

Waitress Phyllis Schink has seen and heard the Pilgrim Hall door open and close, and she has also heard the rest room doors do the same—at times when she was absolutely, positively certain there was no one in either rest room.

"We really don't know," she shrugged, "but we all agree it has to be Charlie. He was a great guy, very involved here, and we never had anything happen until he died."

From his position at the far end of the bar, Anthony Sadowski chipped in his story.

The guy known as "Slugger" has worked at the lodge as a bartender, and has also seen, heard, and felt the presence of Charlie. He said he is sensitive to that sort of thing, since he has lived most of his life in a house that harbored its own ghost.

But, we were there to talk of the Moose ghost.

"I don't know if it's my imagination or not," Anthony said, "but I thought I've seen things go by in the corner of my eye when I was alone in here.

"Yeah, this place definitely has a ghost in it, and I'm convinced it's Charlie."

58

Joe Viola is also in agreement, and like "Slugger," Joe also professes to live in a haunted house.

Joe's place is not far from the Moose Lodge. Almost immediately after moving into their Chestnut Street home several years ago, he and his wife, Marie, started to experience untoward happenings.

Actually, Joe has borne the brunt of the strangeness.

"Weird things started to happen," he said, "like one time I put my eyeglasses on a table. I was nowhere near them and I heard a thump behind me and they were in the middle of the floor.

"Another time I was sitting on the sofa and someone tapped me on the shoulder. And believe me, I know it was a tap on the shoulder. I turned around and there was nobody there.

"That's when I told my wife that we had a ghost in that place!"

It is interesting to note that those incidents–and many other seemingly trivial glitches in Joe's everyday life–only started to take place when they were building an addition to the 100-year old house they had purchased.

That is in keeping with the one strong thread that runs through virtually every story this writer has investigated in more than 20 years of research.

It seems more than coincidence that in each of those stories, some sort of work–rebuilding, renovating, rehabilitating, adding, or subtracting architectural appurtenances–has taken place on the afflicted property.

This disturbance of the plane upon which the psychic energy was accustomed to have inhabited may well have unleashed that energy on unsuspecting mortals. It is part and parcel to what I have come to call the "rusty nail theory."

It is a premise subscribed to by many observers, and a concept I have detailed in previous books.

Upon death, I suggest, what was flesh and bones–the human body–becomes nothing but a spent container, of sorts. But, what were electrical charges in the nervous system may continue as information-laden impulses that stay suspended and circulating in an eternal swirl of a magnetic field.

Could these impulses–these shards of emotions and bits of information leftover from a life–then record themselves somehow, on something?

As in simple video or audio recording, could not these invisible impulses become attracted to and deposited on ferrous oxide–rust?

Could these scientifically rational and conceivable electrical charges which burst from the corporeal confines at the time of extreme trauma–including, but not limited to, death, be the seeds of the supernatural?

Could these bits and pieces be ghosts?

Could the renovations have disturbed that recording by exposing the rust and allowing an unwary psychic mind–such as, in Joe Viola's house–to push the "playback" button and detect those impulses?

As inconceivable as this may be to some, so is the proposition that living faces and forms and voices and sounds could be recorded on strips of rust-coated plastic and retrieved on a glass screen or paper speaker.

But those are the wonders we call audio and video, which in an electronic age seem all so natural.

While discussing Joe's relatively minor incidents in his North Wildwood home, his wife, Marie, asked a question that leads to yet another interesting observation.

It seemed that Marie has actually found it frustrating that she has never experienced any encounter with a ghost, although she would revel in the opportunity.

She finds it particularly disappointing because, for 19 years of her life, her family lived inside the historic German Lutheran Cemetery on Lehigh Avenue in Philadelphia, where her father was a caretaker.

Another major misconception about ghostly activity is that spirits rise to haunt under such atmospheric conditions as "on a dark and stormy night," or "in the glow of the full moon," or "at the stroke of midnight."

As eerily romantic and mysterious as those images may be, it should be remembered that ghosts don't wear wristwatches (scratch, then, the "midnight" theory), and ghosts aren't at all fazed by the phases of the moon or the climatic conditions of our world.

That, as anyone who probes these matters, is a wretched oversimplification.

Suffice to say, in Marie Viola's case, where she resided–inside the walls of a graveyard–would really not make her any more susceptible to supernatural chicanery than anyone outside those walls.

It's all very simple, and is related to what you read a few paragraphs ago.

When that electrical energy bursts from a human being at the time of death and imprints itself as spirit energy, the body remains only as a lifeless shell, a corpse.

Those are what are interred in cemeteries–corpses. The energy is deposited elsewhere.

Or, at least, that's a prevailing and plausible belief.

It is a scary thought–*strolling at the stroke of midnight under a full moon on a dark and stormy night high on a windy hill within the walls of a graveyard*–scary indeed.

But, there is no reason to fear that stroll in that place at that time. No reason at all.

I have taken countless nocturnal walks through graveyards in every weather condition and at every hour of the night.

I know better. I *know* that no skeleton's bony hand will ever push through the soil and grab my leg. I *know* no hollow-eyed ghoul will ever rise from behind a tombstone and leap in my path. I *know* that no horrid demons will swoop from the underbrush and consume my soul.

I know all of this. Still, I tread lightly. I keep a watch over my shoulder, over each tombstone, and behind every tree. My heart pounds, my nerves are on edge–although I know there are no ghosts in any graveyards.

Or…are there?

Such is the magic and the mystery in all of this.

A whimsical ca. 1908 post card depicts the evils of another kind of "spirits" at the Jersey Shore.

THE "SPOOKED ROOM"
OF THE HIGHLAND HOUSE

The Highland House at 131 North Broadway in West Cape May is unique in some ways.

Most notable is the fact that it is a Colonial-style structure, built in the mid-19th century. Its classic design is a bit of a departure from the Victorian flavor that dominates other parts of town.

It is also rare among its Cape May B&Bs because it offers a "Pets Welcome" room specifically situated for the convenience of pet lovers who can't bear to leave their best buddies in a kennel or with a house-sitter.

In fact, innkeeper Dave Ripoli, who shares his life with his puppy "Sunset," dedicates his entire inn on certain off-season weekends to guests with pets.

Those architectural and emotional differences aside, the Highland House is quite like several other Cape May hostelries in that it is abundantly charming and undeniably haunted.

At least two generations of innkeepers won't deny that latter statement.

"I purchased the Highland House in 1994 from an elderly couple," Dave Ripoli said. "At the settlement table, the woman I bought it from mentioned that the place had a ghost. I didn't think much of it at the time. She talked about it as if it was common knowledge. It was sort of light conversation."

Actually, Dave remembered, the talk was of two ghosts a woman and a man they called "the captain." She said the woman's ghost manifested in many ways. As for "the captain," he was identifiable by the distinctive sound of the footsteps of someone wearing what could be described best as a pair of wet boots.

Most realtors, attorneys, or prospective property buyers might agree that the settlement table might not be the best time to bring up the prospect that the place the purchaser is about to spend a lot of money on is haunted—even if it's just "light conversation."

Dave Ripoli was undaunted. Heck, even the bank manager who was present at the closing of the deal knew about the ghosts of the Highland House. But Dave could never have been dissuaded from completing the deal.

At that time, he was a staunch non-believer. At that time.

"I listened to her," he remarked, "but didn't think much of her tales until weeks later when other stories began to surface."

Dave plunged into his project of renovating the inn. While the physical labors proceeded, he became more intimate with his new surroundings.

"Initially, it was just getting used to the house," he said. "One morning, a family of six rang my bell. I thought it was guests inquiring about accommodations but found that they had once owned the property several years ago. I invited them in to see the changes I was making to the house and to get some questions answered as far as what the house looked like when they lived there.

"The six people included three generations; a daughter, mother, and grandmother.

"I was showing them the second floor when the grandmother stopped dead in her tracks in the doorway of one of the rooms. Her granddaughter asked her what was the matter. She answered, 'the room is beautiful, but I'm not going in there. It's the *spooked room*.'

"The granddaughter then said, 'don't you mean haunted?' The grandmother said, 'call it what you want, I'm not going in!'"

In subsequent conversations with a previous owner, Dave discovered that a woman did pass away in the house, and in what the elderly woman called the "spook room."

That "spooked room," which I will not identify by number or name, has been a constant source of, well, spooky activity at the Highland House.

Not long after the three-generation family dropped by, a woman who had stayed there on many occasions in the past came to call on the immediate past owners of the property. When Dave informed her that he had recently purchased it from them, she related yet another tale.

"She told me that she was a regular guest there for a while and that she would travel with her small dog," Dave remembered

"She referred to the same room that spooked the other woman and said that her dog would go into that room, but would bark when he was in the middle of the room and would refuse to go any farther regardless of how much they coaxed and pulled at him."

Eventually, one of Dave's caretakers and he himself would find themselves teased and tested by the energies that seem to swirl in that one room and, perhaps, beyond.

Early on in his tenure there, Dave hired a woman to act as caretaker and serve any guests who may call during the off-season.

"One weekend," he said, "I dropped by and asked her how things were going. She said everything was fine–except for *the ghost*.

"I asked her who told her about the ghost. I told her I didn't, because I didn't want her to be worried about it.

"She said that no one told her. She had a girlfriend over and they were watching television when they heard furniture moving in the room above them.

"At first, she thought I was up there, but she checked the driveway and there was no car there. Of course, I wasn't there."

Nor, he said, was anyone else.

And the room the two women heard furniture shuffling in? The "spooked room," of course.

"Another time," Dave continued, "I had a plumber doing some work there and he told me that he and his assistants also heard the sound of furniture moving in that same room."

As for his own experiences, Dave said his loyal puppy, who follows him everywhere, has occasionally been out of character when she stands at the bottom of the main staircase, cocks her head, barks, and seems to focus her attention on something–or someone–at the top of the stairs. Of course, there is nothing–and no one–at the top of the stairs at the time.

The attic lights have seemingly turned themselves on, and there is an occasional flowery aroma that wafts through the place.

Then, there's the time Dave was working there and decided to settle in for the night in one of the guestrooms. "I laid on the bed and removed my eyeglasses," he said. I was in a sleepy state when I thought I heard a creaking in the wicker settee that was across the room. I knew that there wasn't a draft coming in from the nearby window but couldn't understand what was causing the noise. The light was still on–turning the light off was something I stopped doing several weeks prior to this.

"Anyway, I put my glasses back on and leaned as close as possible to the chair. There was nothing on it, yet it continued to make the noise. I guess it was ten or fifteen minutes later when I decided it was best to go down to the living room and sleep on the couch. I hurried out of the room, leaving the light on…and whatever was behind me. I still can't explain that one."

Oh, yes–the room he *tried* to sleep in?

The "spooked room."

Light House, by Moonlight, Cape May Point, N. J.

THE SHADOW MEN
OF POVERTY BEACH

Because they asked me to, I will never reveal the names of the individuals who told me the tale you are about to read.

Both the young man and his wife are professionals, and the nature of their practices is sensitive enough to warrant their anonymity. In lengthy emails and telephone conversations, their credibility seems unquestionable. I would have no reason to think that what they told me was not the truth.

Still, their story is one of the most baffling I have ever recorded.

The autumn evening was perfect for a walk on the beach. Brilliant bands of amber, crimson and gold swept across the western sky as the sun set on the other shore of the cape and over the Delaware Bay.

A young couple left their hotel in Cape May and headed on the Promenade to stroll into the balmy night.

Dusk was settling in quickly. A gentle breeze kicked in from the ocean. By the time the two reached the end of the Promenade around Madison Ave., she was a bit chilly. He was not. She untied her sweatshirt from around her waist and slid it over her shoulders. The night was too calm, too comfortable, too enticing to return to their room so soon.

They continued on their way in the shadows of the big hotels along Beach Ave., farther and farther until they reached the strand known as "Poverty Beach."

Once a remote and rugged bog beyond Pittsburgh Ave., that land, Sewell Point, was forever changed when the late, lamented Hotel Cape May opened there in 1905.

What was to later be called the Christian Admiral Hotel was demolished in 1996. It may well be that when those walls fell, the ghosts that dwelled within them were unleashed to again alter the sandscape of Poverty Beach.

That, at least, could be one explanation–one baseline–for the strange experience of that young couple on that evening in the fall of 2001.

As they ambled alongside the craggy dunes, the seabreeze stiffened and brought with it a mist that enveloped them in a chilly, moist blanket of air.

The western sky had rapidly faded to black. To the east was the occasional silvery outline of waves rolling onto the sand. A feeble moonlight, and the faint glow from Cape May provided a dim illumination for what was to remain of their nocturnal perambulation.

The couple had veered far from the streetlights of Beach Avenue. They were about to turn around and make their way back along the roadway to their hotel.

And then, it happened.

The young man told the story well in his correspondence:

"We had just decided to make our way back to the hotel when we both were distracted by something off to our left, in toward the street.

"Both of us glanced there, and both of us saw the same thing. What we were looking at were what seemed to be three men. Actually, it was pretty clear that there really were three men standing there. Both of us commented at just about the same time that we wondered who those three guys over there were.

"At first, they were just outlines. We actually kidded around about it. I looked at my wife and sort of kidded to her, 'Ooooh...*shadow men!*

"It did startle us at first, the fact that three men were there, it was getting foggy, and we were in the middle of nowhere. But that was nothing compared to what we watched happen.

"Of course, we kept our eyes on the three men. The mist thickened and lifted briskly, and we could occasionally see that they were standing, and sometimes walking on a dune or rock pile, or something. At least, that's what we thought.

"It also appeared, from what we could see, that each one of them was dressed in a suit and tie. It almost seemed as if they were wearing tuxes and tails, or something like that. That was a little strange, we both thought, given the when and where of things. For the first minute or so that these guys attracted our attention, they also tweaked our curiosity.

"In a little while, as we started walking back to town, we looked over to see that these men were not standing on a dune or anything–they were, and you have to believe us–floating about three feet off the sand.

"In between more dense fogbanks rolling in, we could see these 'shadow men' more clearly. We both realized that they didn't seem to move as individuals. Each one of them seemed to stand erect and motionless. Only as a group did they move, and that was only in a gliding fashion, about three feet off the sand.

"Think what you might at this point, but both of us would swear on a stack of bibles that what I'm telling you is true. And, it gets better!

"The three men, each standing still and shadowy, continued to slowly move, all together as a group. The mist or fog would break from time to time and we could clearly see this very weird little show. Honestly, if I was reading this, I don't think I'd truly understand how strange it all was, and I don't know that I'd believe any of it. But trust me, and my wife–it happened just as I am telling you "

As the couple gazed into the mist, the three gentlemen remained fixed in motionless stances and glided as a trio a few feet off the surface of the beach,

But then, the phenomenon took an even odder twist.

"You must remember that all of this took maybe two or three minutes. It was one of those times, though, that a minute seemed like an hour. We both looked all around to see if someone was playing a trick. We joked that what we were watching almost looked like a low-flying kite in the shape of three men or maybe a cardboard cutout.

"And, just as we agreed to those descriptions, the vision seemed to drift higher off the sand until it swirled rapidly and disappeared higher and higher into the dark sky until we lost track of it.

"We stood there in shock. Our eyes must have been as big as pie plates. Both of us shook our heads and took deep breaths. After pausing a few more minutes and watching the mist grow ever thinner and eventually dissipate, we started our very nervous walk back to our hotel.

"The event kept us up most of the night, speculating as to what we might have seen and what might have caused it.

"So, did we see ghosts? Were our eyes playing tricks on us, or was it all some kind of joke someone was playing on us? We'll never know, I guess."

Quite true, they may never know. However, allow me to suggest one possible source for the manifestation they may have witnessed on Poverty Beach.

The couple placed the site of the sighting of the "shadow men" as somewhere just beyond Pittsburgh

Avenue. That would have been opposite the former Christian Admiral Hotel.

It was on that beach that Louis Chevrolet raced early automobiles. It was in that hotel that Henry Ford and other notables stayed. It was in that hotel that ailing and weary soldiers and sailors were accommodated during both world wars. It was in what boasted as being the "largest hotel in the world" that untold human dramas were played out and unfathomable, perhaps unspeakable events took place.

In short, so much energy was expended in that once-grand hotel that some of it might very well have spilled over to the "other side."

What that couple may have seen was a ghostly tableau swirling in an eternal snapshot, of sorts.

Stationary spirits, ghostly forms that appear, stand motionless, and fade away, are not unusual.

Three stationary spirits, grouped together, levitating several feet off the ground and spinning out of an ocean mist into the night sky—now *that* is unusual.

It is not unreasonable to theorize that the spirit energy of those three men is somehow trapped in a time or place no mortal will ever know until they are cast into it.

Many believe that all psychic energy truly does spiral in sort of an eternal whirlwind. It may orbit in a pattern as tight as a tornado or as wide as a comet. It may make its presence known often or infrequently and be detected with ease or difficulty.

There is no pattern to any of this. There are no profound answers, no black, and no white.

No matter how sophisticated the electronic ghost hunters think their gadgetry may be and no matter how sensitive psychics may believe they are, all of this remains a deep, dark mystery.

I truly hope there will never be too many answers to the unknowns that surround hauntings and ghost stories.

Do ghosts really exist?

Of course they do.

Can it be proven?

Of course not.

And so it shall and should be.

Every day, one more mystery is solved, one more question is answered, one more barrier is broken, and one more frontier is crossed.

We live in an age of "no boundaries," and "no limits." Or, at least we have been led to believe we do.

Our souls have been skinned of the wonderment and, yes, the fears our ancestors must have felt when they experienced phenomena that we in the "enlightened" 21st century have had explained by science and technology.

Worse than that, our imaginations have been pounded and pummeled by the realities of our lives and lifestyles.

I sincerely hope I will never awaken in the morning and read a newspaper headline or hear on the radio that the mystery of ghosts and hauntings has been solved by science.

There are those among us whose imaginations have been so blunted and battered that they can no longer gaze into the night sky and wonder, no longer walk past a graveyard and keep a watchful eye out for ghosts, or walk along a beach on a misty night and accept the unknown.

There are those whose minds are so rational and thoughts so reasoned that they reject the notion of ghosts and hauntings.

Between you and me, let them continue on their way, for they shall never feel what we feel as we pass that graveyard or stroll that beach.

What's more, they'll never get the chill I get when I write these stories—and the chill I hope you get when you read them.

Opened as the Cape May Hotel, this massive structure was last known as the Christian Admiral Hotel before its demolition in the 1990s.

THE LIGHTKEEPER'S GHOST

Diminutive and dignified, the Hereford Inlet Lighthouse stands just a tad over 49 feet high, but in its prime its beacon shone at least 13 miles over the waves.

Its architectural style has been called "Victorian," but it is more specifically "Swiss Gothic."

It was 1871 when a Life Saving Station was authorized for the entrance to the tricky waters of Hereford Inlet. The site chosen was the tiny fishing village of Anglesea (now North Wildwood) on an island known formally as Five Mile Beach.

Very soon after Station #36 opened, the need was clear that a lighthouse was also needed at the inlet.

After the cedar and holly scrubs were cleared, the light and keeper's house were built. What set the

Adolescent and unenlightened tal
places often come up devoid of any tru
Simply put, just because a place *looks* ha
not necessarily mean that it *is* haunted.

As determined by two psychic investigators
lighthouse workers who say they are sensitive to
activity, the Hereford Inlet Lighthouse is not hau
by any intense energy.

This is not to say, however, that there is not a
presence on the *grounds* of the wonderfully landscaped
site.

"I personally have sat on the bench and thought that
something was there," said Betty Mugnier, manager of
the attraction.

She is talking about one particular bench at the
seawall of the grounds.

It is there that a psychic who surveyed the keeper's
quarters and grounds also discovered a presence.

"About the same area where she felt something and
here I thought there was something is where the
sc used to sit," Ms. Mugnier continued.

e first occupant of that house was, of course, the
ighthouse keeper at Hereford Inlet, John Marche.
much is known about him, as he perished in the
inlet when his boat capsized not far from the
g beam that he had tended for only three

elieve the "feeling" that unsuspecting
f members, volunteers, and psychics sense
awall and at one particular bench may be

...aritime outpost apart from others was that the light
...wer and domestic quarters were self-contained.

The Hereford Inlet light beamed for the first time on
May 11, 1874.

In its early years, the facility served both those at
sea and those in the community. The first religious
services ever held on the island were conducted there,
and the lightkeepers were key citizens of the growing
resort and fishing community.

After a savage storm lashed the inlet in 1913 and
threatened the foundation of the lighthouse, it was
moved about 150 feet to the west, where it remains
today. In 1964, the lighthouse was decommissione
and remained derelict until 1982 when concerne
citizens of North Wildwood restored the uniq
facility and opened it as an historic site.

Do ghosts wander within the charming
walls of the picturesque lighthouse?

Strangely enough, no. After all, its line
its five fireplaces, and its hint
"gingerbread" seem to provide the p
haunting or two.

This serves to dispel anothe
how and *where* ghosts may d
There is scarcely a city
that does not have the r
"haunted road" or "ha
More than likely
Gothic kind of p
an Addams Fam

w
hou
T
first
Not
perilous
lifesavi
months.
Some b
visitors, sta
along that se

the ghostly energy of John Marche, trapped forever in the fickle winds and waves of Hereford Inlet.

THE HAUNTING OF CHERRY HOUSE

I n its crisp, gleaming white clapboard Colonial style, and wrapped in a white picket fence, Cherry House seems more suited for a lane just off the village green in a New England town than in the heart of Victorian Cape May. But somehow, it fits quite well.

It has done so since Lemuel Leaming, a descendant of one of the Cape's first families, built it in 1849.

Clearly pre-dating the Victoriana, Cherry House was the home of James Mecray, the first burgess of Cape Island (which, in 1875, became Cape May) and received its common name from the Cherry family that lived there in the mid-20th century.

All of that can be read on an historical plaque in front of the house.

What cannot be seen by the passer-by is the spectacular restoration done by Beth and Frank Acker, who also maintain a residence in Montgomery County, Pennsylvania.

The couple purchased the house as a summer home in the late 1990s and plowed a pretty penny into what had been a rather rundown property. "My husband said we paid a fortune for a fixer-upper," Beth Acker joked.

They knew from the start that much work was to be done. The entire kitchen would be gutted and refitted. The warren of rooms on the second floor would be remodeled. Hardwood floors would be restored, and many other unexpected challenges would lie ahead.

What the Ackers may not have expected would be the challenges of dealing with one, or maybe two, or perhaps even three phantoms within their "fixer-upper."

Just as they knew they had their work cut out for them with the restoration, they learned quite early on that they might share their Cape May dream home with an unseen inhabitant.

"One of the neighbors had hinted to us when we first moved in that the house was haunted," Beth said. "At first, we really didn't have a sense about that."

That neighbor, almost incidentally and certainly innocently, mentioned the alleged haunting as the couple made settlement on the house. But, they were unfazed.

The stories centered on one particular staircase that leads from the second to the third floor. It's a rather short set of steps and leads to a floor the Ackers had not yet fully restored at the time this account was written.

It is on those steps where neighbors, visitors, and previous residents have seen the filmy figures of a young boy and an elderly man.

One neighbor who had heard the stories also heard the ghosts were those of a grandfather and grandson who once lived there and, perhaps, died there.

The story is vague, and the baseline for any haunting is thin. What is certain is that strange things do go on inside Cherry House from time to time, and although Beth and Frank Acker have tried to brush them off, they're having a tougher time doing so—especially as the stories from *others* are told.

Those others include a host of tradesmen who have worked on the restoration project.

"The builder told us the plumber had gone into the library to use the telephone and water started running in the bathroom," Beth recalled.

"And then, through the door came an apparition and it walked right through him! He was totally freaked out!"

Beth laughed as she told the story, but that laughter was within a frame of caution.

The plumber's apparition was probably the most tangible of all reports that came out of the various workers, but it was not the last.

"The builder said the plumber ran out in the kitchen, as white as can be. He would not go back into the room, not even to hang up the phone.

"Another member of the work crew said he came into the house one time and heard us upstairs, walking around. He said he came through the house yelling, 'Hey Ackers, I'm here!' But, of course, we weren't in the house. We were in Pennsylvania."

The notion of someone moving about upstairs is not alien to the Ackers. They have heard such sounds, and have watched as other odd things unfold there.

The bedroom door at the top of the stairs would occasionally open on its own. It's a "summer door," slatted and not prone to swinging in any breeze. Still, breeze or not, it would creak open, leading Beth to accuse Frank and Frank to accuse Beth of opening it–when neither, of course, had.

Once the cross-accusations were resolved, both kept a closer watch on the door. "We would close it before we would walk into town and when we came back, it would be open," Beth said.

Quite possibly the most profound and perplexing episode the Ackers endured took place in the cozy, comfortable library. Just to the right of the front entrance, it is the kind of room every house should have.

"We were sitting in the library one night," Beth remembered, "and it sounded like somebody was rocking in the rocking chair. It was making a lot of noise. We both looked at the chair and then at each other and then at the chair again and said, 'Oh, this is nice, the rocking chair isn't moving!'"

But, the rocking sound continued for a nervous few minutes.

There are always the possibilities–however remote–that a breeze did kick the door open or a shifting of the framework of the house had creaked it open. Maybe the floorboards shifted...or something. There are always those possibilities. But, one look at the door or the floor would all but expunge those explanations.

What the Ackers are left with is the very *real* possibility that the neighbors, and the workers, are right.

Neither Beth nor Frank has ever seen the little boy or the older man. But, as the interview progressed, it seemed to this writer that they wouldn't mind catching a glimpse or two. It might serve to answer a few questions.

"It doesn't bother me," Frank admitted.

His wife was even more cryptic: "I do believe that things get revisited.

"I absolutely love this house. And, I always felt that the house knows that."

📖

YOU <u>CAN</u>
FRIGHT CITY HALL!

Very well, it's not the best chapter title. However, it is somehow appropriate when it refers to the city hall in Ocean City.

As I prowled the South Jersey shore in search of things that go bump in the night, I expected a windy old hotel or two, the occasional restaurant, and a bevy of B&Bs to give up their stories with little effort.

I never expected to uncover a tale of terror in, of all places, the seat of Ocean City's government.

Very well again, "tale of terror" may be a little over the top, but for those who have experienced what one employee there casually called "the guy upstairs," the experiences have indeed bordered on nothing less than terror.

87

I was tipped off to the story by none other than the president of the Ocean City Historical Museum, Inc., Paul Anselm.

"I've been told this by several people who are not prone to exaggerate," Anselm told me. "It's been going on for a number of years."

Indeed, when I placed a call with the city's purchasing agent, his administrative assistant readily recognized the subject of my request. It was she who called it "the guy upstairs" and promised that the purchasing agent would get back to me and provide vivid details of the experiences he and many others have had in the hallowed halls and rooms of the stately structure in the heart of the city.

The story is set in the city council chambers, which occupy the south, ocean side of the building's third floor. But, its eerie echoes reverberate through the workaday offices on the floor below.

"You can hear a door squeak upstairs," Anselm continued. "Then, footsteps, actually going across the hallway that's directly over the purchasing agent's office, and then over other offices.

"These footsteps would then proceed down the steps...and then disappear."

Anselm admits it could be a case of contagious hysteria, but he has heard the same story from several trusted, longtime city hall employees.

"This is not once in a great while," he continued. "It was be repeated, and there is a number of people who would agree that they have heard the footsteps."

Anselm recalled one particular cleaning crew that was so bedeviled by the third floor footfalls that they literally walked off the job and never returned. One crewmember added that as he heard the footsteps, he also felt a very strong and chilling breeze brush by him.

The task of confirming and elaborating on these tales fell on the shoulders of Ocean City Purchasing Director Joe Clark.

Not five seconds into the conversation with Clark, however, he made a firm statement: "I never said it was a ghost."

True, in private conversations with Paul Anselm and in public newspaper interviews about the ghost, er, incidents at city hall, Clark measured his words. "I am always very clear about that," he explained, "because I have never seen anything. I have only heard things."

But, just wait until you read about what he has heard!

Furthermore, although Joe Clark has never witnessed an apparition in the building, he has counseled at least one individual who has.

"There have been noises heard that we cannot attribute to any known source," Clark continued. "Nobody ever said anything for a long time. I would hear it, even walk upstairs–I'm not a person who's fearful of this type of stuff–so I would walk up, not see anything, and then go back to my desk and work."

Still, he would wonder about the very clear and queer sounds that drew him to investigate.

Joe Clark refers to a "we" when he discusses the gho—oops, the *sounds* that have echoed late at night in the big building.

It is a classic case of many hearing much but saying nothing to anyone. Until, that is, a group of coworkers gathered after work and, one by one, each told the other about their experiences.

"I must say," Clark admitted, "that was a little spooky when we all told our stories about things we had heard and the stories were all the same."

Clark pointed out that sounds easily reverberate within the marble steps and tile walls of the afflicted floor. He is quite familiar with the *known* sounds—pipes clanking, things like that.

But then, there are those swinging, clunking doors...and the footsteps.

"There are two doors that go into council chambers," he noted. "They're full-length, saloon-type doors. They make a distinctive sound—they swoosh—when they open and close. I would hear that and then hear footsteps. I would go upstairs, and there would be nothing there."

At one time, he even had an office mate go upstairs on a quiet night and open and close the doors. As Joe listened in his office, he heard the familiar swooshing sound as the nocturnal knocking was perfectly replicated.

The only reported sighting of something in or around those council chamber doors took place sometime in 2000. In his position as Purchasing Agent, Joe Clark was first to get the news.

"The proprietor of the contracted cleaning firm called me and told me, *'You never told us there was a ghost in the building!'*

"Well, I told him I never told anybody there was a ghost in the building, *'Where'd you get that information?'*"

He got the information from a member of the night cleaning crew who fled the building and quit his job after an unpleasant, uncomfortable encounter on the third floor.

"I later spoke to that young man who had left the building," Joe said. "He told me that he had been mopping the floor in the same area we have heard things.

"He said he felt as if someone was standing behind him. He turned and saw what appeared to be an elderly gentleman, somewhat hunched over, walking toward him. And then, the man walked right *through* him!"

The young man has since disappeared into the workforce of another city and could not be reached for comment.

What could be causing the perplexing sounds that have cause several employees at city hall to at least entertain the possibility that a ghost walks the third floor council chambers and corridors?

Built in 1914, the building has housed the town jail, police department, and even the bunkhouse and engine room of the fire department.

There are rumors that the energy that certainly seems to inhabit the structure may be that of a former mayor of Ocean City, but they are only rumors.

What is known is that in its long history, city hall has certainly been the site of countless and sometimes intense human dramas. It could well be that one or more of those have somehow left an indelible imprint for some to hear and one to see.

OCEAN CITY, N.J.

Showing its Unrivaled Location, Beautiful Sea-Shore, Protected Sailing Waters and Famous Fishing Grounds, also Railroad and Ferry Connections. Artesian Water, Sanitary Sewage, Electric Lights, Gas, Electric Cars.

THE PHANTOM OF
THE FLANDERS

It is an architectural and historical gem of the Jersey Shore. It is a survivor, whether as a hotel or as a condominium complex, or in whatever configuration it will be by the time you read this.

93

It is arguably the finest hotel anywhere along the shore between Atlantic City and Cape May.

It is the Flanders, on the Boardwalk at 11th Street in Ocean City.

Designed in the style of a grand European hotel, the Flanders was named after Flanders Fields in Belgium, and Belgian motifs were carried through from the house china to wall decorations. After it opened in the early 1920s, it became a seaside favorite of many leading citizens of the era.

As time, tastes, and trends changed, the Flanders Hotel seemed to become lost in the shuffle of high-end hotels in Atlantic City and low-rise motels elsewhere "down the shore."

Somehow, though, it has survived.

No matter what it was or what it may become, the Flanders will always have one constant–one feature that will forever make this Ocean City landmark very special.

It will always have its ghost.

When I arrived at the Flanders to inquire as to whether there were any ghost stories or legends attached to the place, I was greeted by G. Michael Alber. In his sales office just off the main lobby, Mr. Alber smiled and promptly ushered me up to the elegant second floor.

There, in the broad parlor hallway that connects the various public rooms, I was shown a magnificent portrait of a mysteriously beautiful young woman.

94

The young woman is Emily. Emily is the ghost–the fetching phantom–of the Flanders.

Some call her "The Lady in White."

In fact, beneath the portrait is her story, on a handsome plaque for all to read:

Over recent years, a ghost of a lady in white has often been seen wandering through the Flanders by both staff members and guests.

The most recent sighting was in the basement of the building in the early hours of July 7, 1999. She was described as being in her early twenties with long brown hair. Two earlier sightings were of a similar young woman standing near the grand piano.

The sightings before that were mostly confined to the lady in white walking barefoot through the Hall of Mirrors. On many other occasions, the laughter of a young woman has been heard throughout the building.

Although a ghost, Emily seems happy enough. She's been heard singing and chuckling merrily in many grand rooms of the Flanders.

And so, the story goes.

Who, then, is Emily? How did she come to haunt the Hall of Mirrors, the subterranean chambers known to some workers as "the catacombs," and the brilliant ballrooms of the grand hotel?

Richard Spurlock provided some answers to those questions. A chef who left the Flanders in 2001 "after three wonderful years there," Spurlock spoke of co-workers who told him that they saw, felt, or heard the ghost's presence at the front desk. He remembered others claiming they had heard disembodied footfalls across the floor.

He also remembered one incident that convinced him that the Flanders had an eternal guest.

"I spent some dark, lonely nights at the Flanders," he said. "The one particular thing was when a painting fell off the wall right in front of my eyes. It had been there for better than 40 years. It just fell right off the wall, and it was on there pretty solid. I figured it was the spirit letting me know she was around."

The painting was a portrait of a ship's captain. Could its sudden tumble have indeed been some sort of sign?

Spurlock does not discount that proposition. He said he felt that a lonely, but good presence was in the building during his entire tenure there.

A psychic who "read" the old hotel did detect a strong energy there, in the Hall of Mirrors and in the "Boardroom" which adjoins it.

Although the psychic's findings were held as suspect by most who worked there at the time, she did offer one possible reason the young woman's ghost roams the rooms of the Flanders.

"She believed that she had lost her wedding ring on her honeymoon at the Flanders," Spurlock said, "and that was what was unsettled about her."

Spurlock remembered several other guests and casual visitors who said they had seen or felt something supernatural at the hotel.

"I had a friend who brought a woman in for brunch. She was a Creole woman who was into the voodoo thing. She felt a presence there, as well," Spurlock added.

"Nobody had said a word to her about Emily, nobody told her any of the stories. Yet, right away, she felt that there was the ghost of a young woman there.

"I was a little put back by that."

If there is one person who has been a repository for virtually all of the stories, it is the man who, in a sense, brought the ghost to life.

He is Tony Troy, and it is his work of art that towers elegantly above the placard that identifies the Lady in White.

The Liverpool native fine-tuned his ample talents on the streets of London. He arrived at the Flanders in the mid-1990s at the behest of Jim Dwyer, who had owned the hotel and had taken Tony under his wing.

While Tony was staying at the Flanders, he decided to grace the walls of the ballrooms and other areas with his art.

"The murals are unfinished, as is the portrait of Emily," he said. I'm a street artist from the streets of London. That's where I learned to draw, for the tourists. Somebody gave me the money for an air ticket over here, so I came. I met Jim, and I thought, well, that's one way to leave a legacy, with those paintings."

97

*The "Lady in White" has been spotted gliding through the
Hall of Mirrors at the Flanders Hotel.*

Blending his skills and sensitivities in art and
music with a good portion of imagination, Tony
distilled information and descriptions from the many
stories he had been told about the "Lady in White" and
created the portrait of the ghost named Emily.

"Actually," he said, "I gave her that name. It is just
one of those great old-fashioned names.

"It was all based on fact, though, on all the stories I
had been told. But, when some reporter asked me the
name of the lady, I thought, well, 'Emily.' So, they
just wrote that down and didn't ask any further
questions. I was expecting the next question, 'how did
she come to tell you her name?' But, there were no
more questions. So, the name stuck."

The portrait itself is haunting. The curious, quizzical face of a beautiful, if pale, young woman is framed by billowing brown hair and the creamy dress that gave her the *other* moniker.

Her slender fingers rest on a piano keyboard. She–this "Emily"–seems to be surprised by something.

"It was all based on a few descriptions," Tony continued. "It was a little more romanticized, but generally it follows the stories I was told by several people at the Flanders.

"It was always a girl in a long white dress, usually no shoes, and long, brownish hair. She was described as a bit on the gaunt side."

As the spirit has usually been seen in the Hall of Mirrors or near the grand piano at the end of that gleaming corridor, Tony decided to place his imaginary lady at a piano.

Tony was impressed by the volume, consistency, and credibility of most of the sightings he has been told about. The fact that many people on different shifts and on different jobs in the vast building gave almost the exact same descriptions led him to believe that the stories were sincere.

"Usually it would be late at night," he said. "But, a number of the solid sightings were during the day by people who worked in the kitchen. A lot of them thought it was a real woman. A number of people in the banqueting halls gave me descriptions, as well."

99

As the funnel through which nearly every one of the late 1990s sightings passed, Tony was privy to several tales that still stand out in his mind.

"One of the good sightings," he recalled, "was by one of the workers who was downstairs in the basement. He was opening up a room and saw a girl looking into a toolbox, just gazing over it, as if she was looking for something.

"What was interesting is that the girl turned around and looked at him like *she* was being surprised, and she flitted down the corridor and through the wall!"

He chuckled: "I'm always curious about ghosts who are surprised by humans."

This searching spirit (for a wedding ring, mayhaps?) has turned up on at least one other occasion and in at least one other location.

"Another solid sighting was by one of the girls in the office in the daytime. Again, the ghost, Emily, was looking at framed photographs that were laying on the floor. The girl saw her and screamed, and then the ghost again just went through the wall."

Tony also remembered more vague accounts of the hearing of a young woman's laughter on the second floor, near the Boardroom, and echoing softly in the Hall of Mirrors.

Then, there was the time that one particular individual may have been profoundly affected by the energy that swirls within the walls of the old hotel.

"There was a fireman who walked in and was laughing at the idea of ghosts," Tony said. "But, when he walked into one room, he felt his hair stand on end, he ran out, and refused to go back in. He said there was something in there–he didn't know what it was–but he would not, under any circumstances, go back again."

Has Tony Troy, spiritual father of the common perception of Emily, the Lady in White, ever seen the spirit?

The simple answer is no. But, his interest in things ghostly was peaked when he did see something when he was in his early 20s.

"It was in a 400-500 year old house in Old Portsmouth, England. The family was renting it. Upstairs on the top landing, I saw an old woman. It was about ten o'clock at night. I remember I was getting ready for bed–and my point there is that I wasn't *in* bed–I'm always suspicious of people who say they saw ghosts while they were in bed.

"Anyway, I was just standing by the bed when I saw what appeared to be a kind old woman. I said to her, 'Are you my grandmother?'

"She just smiled and said nothing. The next moment, she just disappeared. And then, I thought, good lord, I'd just seen a ghost!"

Many years later, as his mother, sister, and brother and he were reminiscing about their stay in that house, each of them, for the first time to one another, admitted that they, too, had seen the kind old woman at the top of the steps.

It was Tony's introduction to the world of ghosts.

Neither Tony nor anyone else interviewed regarding the Flanders Hotel story could come up with any firm baseline of the haunting. Just who "Emily" really might be remains a mystery.

"All I know," Tony mused, "is that the sightings have been good sightings from people I have known and would not have expected sightings from."

Vintage views of the oceanfront of the Flanders Hotel, before the Boardwalk expansion.

THE GROWLING GHOST
OF THE MYSTICAL MERMAID

L egend has it that many, many years ago, the basement of the legendary Macomber Hotel on Beach Avenue in Cape May served as a makeshift lockup for those in town who had sampled a bit too much of the bubbly and needed a place to "sleep it off."

This, if true, may account for some of the strange things that have happened inside the lower-level shop now known as The Mystical Mermaid.

Gwen Cavalier is the owner and operator of the shop, and the series of unexplainable events that has unfolded since she opened in June, 2001 prompted her to actually keep a logbook of those incidents.

June 25, 10 p.m.: A dark figure seen moving around in the back hall.

June 26, 8 p.m.: A cold spot, about four feet wide, felt near a counter.

June 27, 7:15 p.m.: A clerk feels someone–or something–tap her on the back in the stockroom.

And on, and on. But, the energies inside the shop made themselves known even before it opened to the public.

"At the very beginning, in April, 2001, when I took possession of the store and started doing renovations,"

103

she said, "Diane Bixler, who operates the ghost tours out of the hotel, came to say hello.

"And, she told me the place was haunted."

Diane also gave Gwen a primer on ghosts and hauntings–what to look and listen for, etc.

"Diane's presence there," Gwen continued, "activated everything, or so it seemed. That day, every time we would put down a hammer, or a paintbrush, or a scissors, we would turn around and it wouldn't be there. My friend who was helping me renovate and was to then work at the store ended up refusing to do so because of those days' events. It freaked her out so badly."

Although a cadre of construction workers and other friends and visitors would sense or see things in her new shop, Gwen was more amused and confused than frightened. Whatever might have been there was more playful than hurtful, she truly believed.

"When we opened the store," she continued, "we began feeling cold spots. We would also hear voices, and sounds."

Those sounds were not of the *whooo-ooo*, garden-variety ghostly groans.

"Our ghost makes animal noises," Gwen claims. "It meows, it barks, it growls!"

A growling ghost? A bit far-fetched? Well, from two very independent and very divergent sources came a possible explanation and a possible confirmation of such a phenomenon.

Purely by chance, a woman who had been on one of the ghost tours informed Gwen about the old stories about the "drunk tank" that once existed in the space now occupied by her shop. She said she had heard of one particular gent–a, shall we say, regular customer–who would spend his nights sobering up and grunting, growling, and making animal noises as he did.

Some say the chap died in an impromptu cell that was located where The Mystical Mermaid is now situated.

He could thus be considered the baseline for the various anomalies that have spooked folks in the hotel basement for many years–and, of course, for the growling.

One investigator who employs digital and analog audio equipment in an effort to capture sounds of spirit energy claimed that his recorders did detect a growling sound. His findings during a technical "reading" of the shop, however, seemed inconclusive.

The abnormal events in the shop also include various and sundry glitches in electrical and electronic devices, employees feeling that they have been tapped on the shoulder, and a few actual sightings.

"What I have seen," said Gwen Cavalier, "is a kind of white, filmy thing that goes by in the corner of my eye. And, there's usually a cold spot accompanying it."

Gwen added, "There have been people who say they have seen a person standing right outside the stockroom door, right near where our bathroom is located. Diane went into the bathroom one night and came flying back into the store and told us she had an encounter in the bathroom."

Diane Bixler confirmed that incident, but said a more harrowing experience for her was the time she watched in awe and uneasiness as a Christmas ball on display in the shop started spinning...and then another...and another...and more–with no air current, no breeze, and no detectable or visible aid. "I'll never figure that one out," Diane said.

Diane has also felt the cold spots that have been so prevalent there. "That is one of the strangest sensations," she added.

Despite the fact that she has led walking tours of haunted sites in Cape May for seven years, Diane is always on the lookout for rational and practical explanations of seemingly irrational and inexplicable events. Sometimes she finds those explanations; most times, she does not.

"Those spinning Christmas balls," she admitted, "will always have me wondering."

Cold spots, electronic hitches, missing tools, taps on shoulders and the occasional apparition aside, Gwen Cavalier believes her shop is haunted by a non-threatening spirit, and is not at all frightened by it.

Even if it could be the ghost of a growling old drunk!

📖

THE LADY IN BLUE

Before we go any farther, let us echo the urgings of the innkeeper of the grand and gracious Candlelight Inn in North Wildwood.

"We don't want to be known as a ghost house," said Bill Moncrief, "It's one of our concerns."

Now, let us echo the sentiments expressed in the guest book at the Candlelight Inn:

...Our stay was like visiting the home of a good friend...

...You have managed to capture some of the Old World charm and calm of yesteryear...

...No place could be as relaxing, comfortable, and peaceful...

Enough said on both counts. Now, to the matter at hand–the "lady in blue" that may be a permanent guest at the beautiful Queen Anne Victorian inn at 2310 Central Avenue.

Mr. Moncrief is a no-nonsense kind of guy, not susceptible to flights of fancy or random claims of "bumps in the night." After all, he was a 20-year Naval aviator, and in his "retirement" worked for a law firm, a federal agency, and even the Center for Science in the Public Interest (a.k.a. CSPI or "The Food Police") before he and wife Nancy became keepers of the Candlelight Inn. Another relevant quote from Bill regarding his latest venture: "CSPI recipes are not being followed in the inn!"

The pedigree of the Candlelight Inn is reflected in its designation as a Select Registry "Inn of Distinction"–one of only 13 in all of New Jersey to earn that honor.

But, back to the "lady in blue."

"Supposedly," Bill said, "the wife of the original owner loves the inn so much that she has not left, even though she is long deceased."

That original owner was Leaming Rice, whose family was very prominent in North Wildwood and beyond.

"The previous owners of the inn told me that they had a psychic stay here, and the psychic actually had a conversation with her and was able to describe her attire. It was similar to what people who knew her said she would have worn in her time," he added.

Her time was the turn of the 20th century, shortly after the home was built in 1905. Mrs. Rice is remembered as a founder of the local Women's Club and a well-respected lady about town.

Her attire, according to the psychic, was a blue dress.

"I haven't witnessed anything myself," Bill Moncrief continued, "but we did have a guest say that she saw a blue apparition in her room."

All well and good, but Bill had to qualify this particular "spirit" sighting.

"While the person who said they saw the blue apparition was very sincere," he stressed, "it was also her and her husband's anniversary. She did admit to have had two bottles of wine, and we had put a bottle of champagne in their room, so we were a little skeptical about it."

Bill added that the room has curved glass windows that may have refracted a blue glow. "And," he continued, "she said hat the apparition later swirled above her. Well, that room also has a ceiling fan."

Bill said that while this "blue apparition" glided through their room, the husband stayed up almost all night–their anniversary night–with camera in hand, trying to capture an image of the apparition on film, to no avail.

There have been other accounts that give Bill pause as he discounts any spirit energy in the Candlelight Inn.

A housekeeper has told him that she often will find a stray penny or two somewhere in a room after she has meticulously cleaned the room. "That happens perhaps a dozen times a year," he said. "She thinks there's something there."

But one reporting did provide Bill with some more solid food for thought.

"My sister-in-law, who is the vice-president of a bank in Manhattan, and thus not prone to exaggeration, was going upstairs and said she saw someone go by her. She realized right away, there shouldn't have been anyone else in the house at the time.

109

"She tried to follow the person into the parlor and then the dining room and when she got into the dining room, there was no one there."

One more set of circumstances, however abstract, has made Bill wonder.

The man who built the house, Leaming Rice, was the city's civil engineer at the time.

Bill and Nancy Moncrief are the third generation of owners of the property. And, at the time Mr. Rice was the civil engineer in North Wildwood, Bill Moncrief's grandfather was the civil engineer just up the coast a bit in Ocean City.

"So," Bill mused, "you never know if there's any meaning to that."

And oh, that couple who celebrated their anniversary in one of the charming rooms of the Candlelight Inn? She who was distracted by the "blue apparition" and he who tried all night to photograph it?

They've booked a return stay.

THE READING ROOM GHOST

I f the Albert Stevens Inn, 127 Myrtle Avenue, Cape May, looks very special with its classic lines and handsome "witch's hat" turret, it is for good reason. It was actually a wedding present!

The namesake of the inn was Dr. Albert Stevens, a homeopathic doctor who had the house constructed in 1898 as a gift for his wife, Bessie.

After Albert and Bessie's only child, Vesta, passed away in 1980, the luxurious residence was sold and soon converted into a bed and breakfast inn, and the architectural splendor of the home was maximized.

Did a ghost or two remain behind?

Lenanne and Jim Labrusciano, innkeepers of the Albert Stevens, do not discount that possibility.

"During the summer of 2001," Lenanne said, "we had a guest who stayed in what was the doctor's reading room. She said that during the night she saw two women in the room—ghosts.

"The only people I thought it could have been would have been the doctor's wife and/or his daughter. The daughter, Vesta, inherited the house and lived here until she passed away."

That same woman, who Jim described as a "self-proclaimed clairvoyant," regaled other guests with her revelations, and assured all that the spirits were of a gentle sort.

"Then," continued Lenanne, "the same young woman was in the dining room, which used to be the doctor's waiting room. She said she felt something there, too, that there were ghost there, as well."

Other guests have hinted to the Labruscianos that they have felt presences in various rooms of the inn. And, there is an interesting twist to some of those reports, including one by Lenanne herself.

"I have heard noises in what was the doctor's reading room," she admitted. "And, as I heard them, my dog started growling, so I don't know."

That may fit a certain pattern. The previous innkeepers were cat aficionados and used images of cats and kittens in their marketing efforts.

There was one report by a guest that they heard what they described as the sound of cat's paws creeping softly across the floor of a certain guest room—the cozy chamber that was once Dr. Stevens' reading room.

There are no cats—no living cats—gracing the floors of the Albert Stevens Inn.

There is, however, one room that retains the former owners' love of felines. It is the doctor's old reading room, the room in which the cat's crawling sound was heard, and the room in which Lenanne's dog growled for no *apparent* reason. It is a room still called, simply, "Cats."

ACKNOWLEDGMENTS

NEWSPAPERS, BOOKS, ETC.

The Press of Atlantic City,
The Courier-Post; Cape May County Gazette; *Cape May County Story* (George F. Boyer and J. Pearson Cunningham, Avalon Publishing Co., 1975); *Cape May County: The Long Island of Philadelphia* (Cape May County Promotion Committee, 1910); *The History of Avalon* (Avalon Home & Land Owners Assn., 1992)

ORGANIZATIONS

Ocean City Historical Museum, Cape May County Library, Lower Cape Branch; George E. Boyer Historical Museum, Wildwood; Library of Congress; Wildwood Crest Historical Society and Museum; Cape May County Department of Tourism; County of Cape May Division of Culture & Heritage; Cape May County Chamber of Commerce; Wildwood Historical Society; Sea Isle City Historical Museum; Avalon Public Library; Sea Isle City Historical Museum; Mid-Atlantic Center for the Arts.

INDIVIDUALS

Edward N. Carson, Doris Hanna, Jane Doherty, Kenny Biddle, Craig McManus, Scott Swift, Harry Otto, Marion Talese, Colleen Dwyer, Terri Adams, Nicki Hartzel, and many others who provided spiritual and inspirational assistance but whose names were not recorded.

ABOUT THE AUTHOR

Charles J. Adams III is a native of Reading, Pennsylvania, where he resides today.

He is the morning air personality on radio station WEEU/830AM in Reading and is a travel writer at the *Reading Eagle* newspaper there.

Adams has served on-camera and in consulting roles for programs on ghosts and hauntings for the History Channel, Travel Channel, The Learning Channel, and MTV. Stories taken from his two-dozen ghost stories books have also been reprinted or adapted for use in major publications and motion pictures.

In constant demand as a speaker and storyteller, Adams has been interviewed or lectured in several states, Ireland, and South Africa, and has led ghost tours to England and Scotland.

A member of the board of directors of the Historical Society of Berks County, Pennsylvania for nearly 25 years, Adams has also served as president of the Reading (PA) Public Library. He is active in many social and civic associations in his hometown, and is also an accomplished musician and songwriter.